SNEAKING AROUND
WITH# 34

PIPER RAYNE

Cover Design: Okay Creations

1st Line Editor: My Brother's Editor

2nd Line Editor: Joy Editing

Proofreader: My Brother's Editor

About Sneaking Around with #34

I have a reputation for being tight-lipped. You learn quick when you become a professional hockey player to be guarded with the media, so I've worked hard to cover up the mistakes of my youth.

But when I'm traded to the Florida Fury, where my ex–best friend is the starting right wing, I'm forced to confront my past. Ford and I have a lot of history, especially when it comes to his little sister, Imogen.

My heart still lurches in my chest when I see her.
My hands want to reach out and touch her.
My mouth wants to keep apologizing.

She's the only woman who ever made me want more. But she's also the one who fell victim to my most regrettable decision.

I'm not a believer in fate, but I must be back in her world for a reason. I've fought for everything I've gotten and I'm not backing down from what I know will be the best thing in my life.

Sneaking Around *with* #34

CHAPTER 1

"It's the wedding crasher."

Warner

$\mathcal{A}$t the start of every season, I'm usually the first player at the rink. Mostly because the months off with nothing on my schedule drives me crazy. I've tried to pick up hobbies, but nothing quiets my brain like skating and pushing the puck around the ice. It's been the sole focus of my life for a long time.

This year is different though.

Last year, I was traded to the Florida Fury midseason, so I'm still one of the new guys in the locker room. Which normally wouldn't be a problem. I'm easygoing and a great player, so I've always gotten along with my teammates. I'm usually well respected. But Ford Jacobs plays for Florida Fury. And Ford Jacobs would love to murder me with his bare hands. And after what I did... I don't blame him.

Ford, I can deal with. His angry outbursts toward me when I miss a play, his wanting to point out all my mistakes to our fellow teammates I can handle. It's another Jacobs who is the cause of my lack of enthusiasm about starting this season.

Ford's sister, Imogen, should be living in New York City where a woman like her belongs. But instead, she's now a Florida resident because she's finished grad school and is trying to figure out her life and hey, why not do it in proximity to her prick of a brother and his baby girl? Every night I'm alone in my bed, it takes every ounce of willpower I can muster not to drive down to her place on the beach, fall to my knees, and beg her to give us another chance.

But unless I want to be the reason Florida Fury doesn't perform well this season, I have to stay far away from her. The last time I was around her was at Ford's daughter's birthday party and we ended up in a bedroom together. I'd just wanted to talk to her, apologize and explain myself, but for a moment, we were back to being those two kids meeting in secret and unable to keep their hands off one another. But it didn't take long for her to snap back to reality, and her eyes flared with her true feelings for me, confirming that I'm the monster she'll never trust again.

I have to put all that aside though. I'm the new guy and this is my job. I cannot fuck up and put my livelihood in jeopardy—my mom and my siblings depend on me. Sure, I have accounts set up for each of them that should cover their college tuition and my mom's living expenses for a good part of her life, but after living without a financial safety net for too long, I know you can never have enough set aside.

Just another reason Imogen Jacobs will never be mine again. I can't fight for her like I want to, because there's just too much for me to lose.

I grab my bag from my truck and head into the Florida Fury arena. Walking down the hallway toward the locker room, I hear the voices of my teammates echoing off the walls. I'll admit one thing, it's the best locker room I've ever been a part of. The razzing and joking and the camaraderie between the guys are awesome. They each have each other's backs. I haven't been part of something like this since high school, when Ford and I played together.

Not that I'm really part of it.

I walk in and the locker room falls silent, all eyes on me. See what I mean? I'm far from a card-carrying member of their inside jokes and fun, but I'm hoping with more ice time and more points on the board, they'll respect me.

"It's the wedding crasher," Tweetie, previously my biggest competition for starting left wing, breaks the silence.

A few weeks back, the higher-ups told me I'll be replacing Tweetie on the starting lineup this season. That second half of last season was a test, and I won. I don't know if Tweetie knows yet but he will after today's practice when he's on the second line.

The wedding crasher comment is in reference to the fact that I ended up at the same resort as Ford and his entire wedding party over the summer. Every player was invited except for me, so when I found out they were there, I was gonna leave and be the ostracized ogre Ford intended me to feel like—until I saw Imogen wearing a bikini.

Hey, I made it clear, my willpower is made of tissue paper when it comes to her.

Then Ford got wind of my presence and made his displeasure known.

"What's up, Langley?" Cory nods.

Cory is a rookie, but we were traded to the Fury at the same time, so I head in his direction. The last three lockers are for me, Cory, and a veteran player, Kane, who was traded last year when people assumed he was going to retire.

"Hey, guys." I drop my stuff and ignore the bad vibes on the other side of the locker room.

"Ready for warm-ups?" Cory asks.

We met up a few times during the off-season, did some drills. Unfortunately, Cory knows that his time on the ice will probably be minimal since Aiden Drake holds the same position in the starting lineup. But I reminded Cory that he needed to be ready should the time come, which it will. Take this time to develop his skills some more, get more experience and confidence on the ice. Drake is only growing older, and it feels like every year in hockey ages you in dog years.

"Yeah." I blow out a breath and get all my shit organized in my locker.

Coach comes in five minutes later, when most of the guys are already suited up. I'm just getting my skates laced. Coach focuses on me for a beat longer. I'm the one who has something to prove. They're giving me an amazing opportunity with the starter position, and if I want to continue to have a hockey career, it's time to put my shit with Imogen to the side and concentrate on what matters. I should've been here earlier, not dragging my feet.

He claps and addresses the room. "We're going to do warm-ups, then Mr. Gerhardt wants to talk to you all."

"Is this about his daughter taking over?" Ford is the only one who has the nerve to ask if the rumors that have been passed around in the off-season are true.

"Just be ready to behave and not act like a class full of kindergartners." He turns his back on us and heads out the doors toward the ice.

ALL OF US head to the ice rink, where the coaches have us do our first conditioning drills since we left. Most of us get workouts in during off-season, but there are always a few who use their time off as a vacation. I'm shocked to discover that this year, it's Ford who's the turtle. He's barely able to catch his breath between drills. I guess love and marriage have changed Ford's priorities.

"Richie, did you do anything at all in the off-season?" Maksim yells, his skates digging into the ice before he heads in the opposite direction.

"I focused on a very specific kind of workout," Ford jokes, which we all know already since he's recently married.

"You have all that time with a kid in the house?" Maksim asks.

"It's called nap time. Wait until you finally have one."

Coach's whistle blows and we all stop and face him.

"Okay, boys, Mr. Gerhardt is on his way down."

But before Coach can finish whatever he was going to say, Mr. Gerhardt and his daughter, Jana, walk around the rink with Imogen following a few steps behind. Every muscle in my body tenses. What is she doing here?

Coach either hears them or senses them because he looks back over his shoulder. "Well, never mind, here he is."

"Thanks, Vittner." Mr. Gerhardt claps him on the shoulder. "Hello, boys."

"Mr. Gerhardt," we all say in unison.

He's probably one of the most feared owners in the league. Tends to not listen to the advisers he hires but goes on instinct, which has to be why I'm standing here right now. All of his scouts must've warned him that putting Ford and me on the same team could ruin the team dynamic needed to win hockey games.

"You all know my daughter, Jana." He motions to her on his left.

Jana steps forward. She's the epitome of dress for success. Nice pantsuit, hair and makeup are flawless, and she's wearing stilettos. "We're so happy to be here for the start of another season. I have a few announcements to make, and before any of you ask, no, I'm not taking over for my dad. But I will be handling a few more things around here."

The entire time Jana is speaking, my eyes soak in Imogen. Just like always, I feel her presence. It's like a living breathing film that coats my skin when she's near.

She's wearing her blonde hair long and straight and has on a professional dress that hugs her curves. Her blue eyes, like her brother's, sparkle, even if they're dodging mine. Instinct tells me it's trepidation at being so near to me. I have the same effect on her as she does on me.

"Most of you will know Imogen as Ford's sister, but she's now our new hype girl. God knows she understands all those apps better than me, and I'm smart enough to hire people smarter than me."

A groan echoes through the empty arena. I glance over to find Ford's gaze lasered in on me. He's probably worried because we both know at some point I'll have to work with Imogen. I'm a hot commodity the team paid top dollar for, a new face for the franchise. Not being arrogant, but my bastard of a father passed down one helluva face, so I know they'll likely want to make my presence known with the public.

I turn my head and face the team owner again.

"With all due respect, what about Barbara?" Ford asks. "Surely she could handle the hype?"

Jana narrows her eyes at Ford. "Imogen works under me. Barbara is now assisting my father."

"I thought she had some great ideas," Ford keeps going, and Imogen's back grows stiffer.

"Ford," Imogen says with a tone of *shut the fuck up, you're going to ruin this opportunity for me.*

Jana crosses her arms and challenges Ford. "If memory serves, she had you visit a senior center last year."

"And they loved me. I guarantee I made fans. And what else do they have to do there but to watch hockey?"

"Did you read the literature on the senior center she sent you to? How about the sign outside?" Jana tilts her head.

"Of course." Ford's arrogance is what drew me to him as a friend in high school and he clearly hasn't lost any of it.

"Then don't you think it's a problem that it was a memory care center? Meaning the minute you walked out, they probably forgot why you were even there."

Ford scoffs.

I wouldn't mind getting to know Jana. Anyone who isn't afraid to go toe to toe with Ford is worth knowing.

The team snickers and laughs. Imogen glances up, and our eyes catch for the briefest moment before she diverts her gaze.

"I'll have meetings this weekend. Some of you will do more heavy lifting than others in the marketing department, as always. Please remember that the contracts you signed included the stipulation of dealing with the media. Imogen has already brought up some great competitions before the games start, and with Coach Vittner's approval, one of you might be asked to participate. Please know if you give Imogen trouble, I will go big sister on you." She eyes Ford.

"I can't imagine if she ever takes over this empire," Kane whispers to me. "She'd have us all in tutus, skating down the rink in some speed competition."

I glance over. "Do you know her?"

"I know *of* her, and that's enough."

I nod.

Mr. Gerhardt claps his hands in front of himself. "That's it, everyone. Let's get 'em, boys. This is our year. I've bought you some great talent with Langley, Freeman, and Burrows, and I have no doubt with their addition to the team, we're gonna bring home the Cup."

No one says anything, and he turns to head back up to his office.

"Go, Florida Fury!" Jana pumps her fist in the air, and it looks robotic, but everyone cheers.

I watch the three of them head out single file. Okay, well, I watch one backside more than the others. It's a secret pleasure. Like sneaking one of the mini chocolate bars out of the candy dish at the doctor's office.

"Fuck, did he seriously just say that?" Cory whispers next to me.

"Yeah, talk about a target on our backs," Kane says.

"Okay, let's try a new line. Freeman, center, Langley, left wing, and Kane, goalie. We'll add Train as right wing. Let's see what you guys have."

We all skate to our positions. I'm not surprised that we're skating against Aiden Drake, Ford, and Tweetie. The Gerhardts might as well have put signs on us that say we're each other's biggest competition. This can only end badly.

"I'm begging you to hit me," Ford says to me at the line. "One hit and I'm gonna knock out your teeth."

"We're teammates now, remember?"

He scoffs. "Don't remind me."

Drake and Freeman jockey for the puck and the fun begins.

Too bad my mind is too preoccupied with Imogen to prove my worth on the ice.

CHAPTER 2

"I swear there's nothing there."
—Imogen

Imogen

"**W**hoa!" Jana shuts the door of her office after we return from the ice rink. "Okay, I've heard some rumors, and I saw the fight at Ford's wedding, but I've never felt that."

Her office is all girl boss with gold, pink, and black decor. Signs on the walls read Hustle, Grind, and Execute, along with other motivational sayings. She walks over to her mini-fridge and pulls out two cans of sparkling water, then meets me at her white couch.

"Felt what?" I ask, accepting the sparkling water. This job is my chance to make something of myself without using my family name, and although I love Jana and she's more friend than boss, I don't want her thinking I'll be distracted by Warner. Especially since I have a meeting in an hour with Mr. Gerhardt to discuss how to make Warner Florida Fury's "it man."

She stares at me with wide eyes as she opens her can. "Don't pretend with me. I'm older and wiser, remember?" After slipping off her heels, she tucks her legs under her as if we're about to have girl time.

I love the way Jana can move seamlessly between professional businesswoman to a girl's girl. Maybe that's why I feel a kinship with Jana. She's so much like my friends back home in New York. Friends I was never able to be honest with about what actually happened between Warner and me.

"Come on. If you don't tell me what's going on with him, then you're fired."

I balk, and she laughs.

"I'm kidding, but I am here if you need me. You look like you need to talk."

I sip my sparkling water, the raspberry flavor a delight. "We just, um... well, he was Ford's best friend in high school."

She waits with her eyebrows arched toward her hairline. "Everyone knows that. There's so much speculation about why they hate each other."

"I'd say Ford hates Warner. I'm not sure Warner ever hated anyone."

Jana licks her lips as though I gave her some bit of juicy gossip to nibble on. "Especially not his best friend's sister."

I shrug, sipping my drink to distract myself. Or act like maybe she's right, but I'm not confirming either way.

"I mean, I'm an only child, but I always wanted an older brother who had friends. Friends who looked like Warner Langley."

"Uh-huh." I sip my water again.

"Okay, I see you're not into this, but if you need to talk, let me know. Ask Paisley. I'm a good friend, and I can tell when someone needs one." Sitting back up, she slips her perfectly manicured toes back into her heels. "Hate to break it to you, but we have to go through some marketing things that involve the man."

"Please don't think I'm unable to handle the job. I can be around him. It's not a problem."

She stops behind her desk, grabbing a remote that shuts

the shades of her office and brings a big screen down from the ceiling. She presses some buttons on her computer and an image of Warner from when he was drafted shows on the screen. My heart plummets like an elevator with the cables cut. I was not prepared to see him like this, because that eighteen-year-old kid is the boy I fell in love with in what seems like another lifetime.

"I'm thinking about really digging deep into his story, so it's good that you know him."

"What?" My voice is quiet because the last thing Warner would ever want is anyone digging around in his past. He keeps that part of his life quiet, and even if I don't check up on what's going on in his life now, it's clear that he still keeps the ones he loves out of the spotlight.

"Did you know there's barely anything about him anywhere? Sure, he graduated from the same Upper East Side Manhattan private school as you and Ford, but other than that, nothing. I think we need to dig deeper with our guys. What made them want to play hockey? Who did they look up to as kids? What is their family like and who are the loved ones they left behind? A deep dive to pull on the heartstrings. Warner has that *boy next door who grew up into a sexy man* vibe that'll put butts in seats and sell merchandise." She sits down and a video plays of an interview he did shortly after he was drafted.

In the clip, he's humble and kind and the arrogance that this league has instilled in him hasn't been developed yet, but I still see a glimpse of his cocky side from being the popular kid in high school... at least until everything went to shit. Everyone thought they knew him, but they really didn't. While Ford went to college, Warner was drafted into the pros. I wonder what it must have been like for him to be thrust into the spotlight at that age after everything that went down in his senior year at school.

"God, he's a magnet. Guys are gonna want to be him and women are going to want to fuck him," Jana says.

I quietly drink my seltzer water, pushing back the memories from that time in my life. A time when I felt as though everything I'd lived for was stripped away. It wasn't until years later that I realized that's the power of young love.

As Jana talks about what a marketing dream Warner is, I'm reminded of the first time I saw him. Hell, the first time I heard someone speak his name, I knew there was something special about him.

I WAS JUST LEAVING American lit when Cici hooked her arm through mine and leaned in close, lowering her voice. "New guy. Senior. Warner Langley. I bet his family owns Langley Wines."

If he was a senior, that meant he was Ford's age, which also meant my brother would make sure to tell the new guy I was off-limits. Ford had restrictions about who I dated—I could only date sophomores or younger. No one older than that because he said then I'd be going into his territory. I swear he's like the rescue pug Mom brought home for Morgan once. He peed on everything from plants, to furniture, to people's legs. Nothing was safe in our house. Rest in peace, Wrinky.

"How hot are we talking?" I asked.

Cici looked around and leaned in so close I could smell her strawberry ChapStick. "I haven't actually seen him yet. Eloise told me he was in her chemistry class. Quiet, sat in the back, but tall, built, and a set of mysterious eyes." She giggled.

"He can't be that hot. And I've never heard of a Langley." I stopped at my locker and opened it.

"I just told you, Langley Wines."

I'd heard of the brand. My parents owned some bottles.

"I don't know. No way he's that hot." I looked at myself in the mirror and reapplied my berry lipstick. In the middle of puckering my lips, Cici nudged me, and I stood straight.

"There he is," she whispered.

I turned and locked eyes with Warner.

Jumbled words floated in my head, and I was unable to form a coherent thought. The boy was drop-dead gorgeous. He had it all, even in Lauder's uniform of khaki pants, white shirt, plaid tie, and blue blazer. Somehow it looked droolworthy on him.

The instant a smile crept over his lips, a rush of heat traveled down my body. With a cocky nod in my direction, he passed by us.

As soon as I heard the voice when he passed, all the marshmallow gooeyness in my body transformed to stone.

"That's my little sister, so it goes without saying... turn your fucking head around unless you want it shoved into the lockers."

Ford was beside him. I hadn't even noticed.

"Ford, you're such an asshole," Cici called to him.

He flipped her off and the two of them turned the corner, heading down the stairs.

"I swear, one day I'm going to dropkick your brother on his ass."

She hadn't known then that it was Warner she'd end up wanting to dropkick.

"Hello!"

I blink and look at Jana, who's all smiles.

"I lost you for a minute there. Still not ready to give me all the deets on what went down between you and Warner?"

Jana seems trustworthy, but she's also my boss—my *new*

boss—and I am not going to pull out old baggage that could jeopardize my new position. The minute she offered me this job when we were at Ford's wedding, I felt it in my soul that this position was meant for me. After getting an art history degree, working some at Jacobs Enterprises, and never finding anything that lit me up inside, somehow this woman in front of me knew before I did that this was the position for me. If I tell her about my history with Warner, she's sure to bring it up with her dad. And one thing I know about Mr. Gerhardt is that the boys on the ice always come first.

"We just went to school together. I was just remembering when he transferred in. He was definitely the 'it man' on campus."

"So he's always been charismatic? I kind of hoped he was some nerdy guy turned hot jock." She laughs and sips her drink.

"Nerdy guy, no. Never." I shake my head.

"Okay, I told you my thoughts. What are you thinking?"

I glance at my empty page. Damn it all to hell. This is not a good start. I rack my brain for anything she might bite on.

"Well, right now I'm assuming men are primarily the ones who buy the tickets and the merchandise, but if we can get their wives or girlfriends involved, it should increase profitability and demand. Then we've expanded our market. Maybe we even have a chance to get groups of women talking about the Fury the same way they talk about *The Bachelor* the day after it airs. And what's going to get a woman who isn't a hockey fan into the arena? A gorgeous guy with a good story. But they have to get to know him."

She nods. "I like the direction you're heading, but be more specific."

Feeling my confidence push to the surface, I go on.

"They need to see interviews with him. Candid ones, and not just the usual ones where he uses all the hockey lingo about getting pucks deep and creating traffic in front of the net. They need to see more, like how he handles himself when he's not prepared. Impromptu stuff. Like meet and greets. Fun social media videos. Win a date and donate to a charity. He can pick a charity and talk about why it's so important to him."

She points her pen at me and starts scribbling. "I love this."

"Are you sure he'll agree to it? The Warner I used to know was pretty private." I hate to bring it up, but I'd hate even more for us to do all this leg work just for him to give us a big fuck you.

"My dad is clear with anyone who joins the team—they are to participate in any marketing activity we request, within reason. I think there's a meeting scheduled with him tomorrow, so we'll go over all this then. If you could really hammer out these ideas tonight, what they'll look like, how we'll pull them off, we'll go over them in the afternoon and present them to my dad and Warner right before the team flies out to Chicago."

"Sure thing." I stand from the couch.

Jana continues, smiling at me. "Last chance?"

I shake my head. "I swear there's nothing there."

At least not anymore. That's what I'll tell myself for the rest of my life. Sometimes people don't come into your life for any other reason than to teach you a lesson. And Warner Langley taught me never to trust a man.

CHAPTER 3

"I'm sorry, but I have to decline the offer."
-Warner

Warner

On my way to the arena for a preseason game, my phone rings through the Bluetooth in my car. Seeing my mom's name flash across the screen, I press Accept.

"Hey, Ma," I answer.

"Warner, honey. How is Florida?"

"Warm. How's New York?"

She laughs. "Cold. Had our first snowfall last night. Just a dusting, but you know how much Julien loves it. He was trying to catch the snow in his mouth."

"Wish I was there." I hit the blinker to make a right.

My phone dings a second later. "Just sent you the video."

"Thanks, Ma."

I'll have to wait until I'm not driving to watch my youngest brother catch snowflakes on his tongue. He's loved snow since he was little and I'm glad to see that being eleven hasn't changed him that much. In a few years, he'll be too cool for that.

"No problem."

There's a pause while I change lanes, then I ask, "Any other reason for the call?"

"Just curious how things are going." She chuckles

because we both know what she's doing—prying for information.

"They're good. Ford's a prick as usual, but there are two other guys on the team that I hang with. Don't worry about me."

"You're my baby boy, of course I'm going to worry about you. And you know who I'm talking about, so stop dodging the question and give me the deets." I hear a lot of noise behind her, so I assume she's cleaning the house or preparing a meal.

"Deets? Don't tell me Trinity has you abbreviating all your words."

Trinity is my younger sister. She's still in high school and thinks she's the shit.

"You're still dodging."

"I'm not dodging."

I am dodging.

My mom knows the entire story of what went down with Imogen and me. She was the only person in my life at the time that I could trust—besides Imogen.

"How is she?" Her voice lowers and I know she's done with the runaround.

I sigh. "Still hates me. Don't blame her."

I have a meeting this afternoon with Mr. Gerhardt, and he mentioned Imogen and Jana might be there, which I'll admit got me to dress better, put on some cologne, and style my hair. I wore my best suit, using the excuse of traveling to Chicago to play tonight.

"Trinity showed me Imogen's social media. She's just as beautiful as she was in high school."

I huff. She's even more so. She's transformed from a cute schoolgirl into a sophisticated woman. Imogen was always confident in herself—it's what attracted me to her in the beginning—but now she carries herself like a woman who knows her worth.

But I don't say that to my mom. Instead I say, "Yeah."

"I have faith. I saw Udessa last night, and she said my family is going to grow."

Jesus, she's always hoping for some wisdom from her tarot-card-reading friend. Let's just hope Udessa doesn't mean our family is going to grow because my mom gets pregnant. Julien was an oops. Hell, so were Trinity and me.

"Tell Udessa she has no idea how stubborn a Jacobs can be. Imogen won't even talk to me." Except for the make-out session we had at Ford's months ago. I still lie in bed thinking about how soft her lips are.

"She predicted you getting drafted. And also your trade." I can picture my mom's back going straight with protectiveness for her friend.

"She said she saw something new on the horizon for me." I flick on my blinker and ease into the left turn lane.

"Yeah, the trade."

"It could've been anything. It could've been a new stick or pair of underwear."

"She said horizon and new. Of course she saw Florida. It all came together when you got traded."

Thank goodness Mom's not here to see me roll my eyes. Udessa is always vague enough that almost anything could be one of her predictions.

"Well, don't count on anything with Imogen and me." I pull into the parking lot of the arena, and I park next to Imogen's Range Rover. She's walking into the building, wearing a deep-green suit. The pants rest right above her ankle, showing off heels I know she paid a fortune for. One thing about Imogen is that she doesn't skimp on fashion. "I gotta go. I'll call you after my game in Chicago."

"Be careful and lead with your heart, Warner. Your heart doesn't lie."

"Okay, Mom, love you. Tell Trinity and Julien I love them too. Bye." I hang up while she's midsentence. I feel guilty for being a shit son but rush out of my car, jogging toward the building in an effort to catch up to Imogen.

I catch the door before it shuts after Imogen and she startles, her hand falling over her heart.

"Hey," I say.

She turns on her heel to head to the elevators. "Hi."

We both wait outside the elevator. She watches the numbers going down as though it's the clock before midnight on New Year's Eve. Except she's not going to kiss me. She's probably going to slide into the elevator and forbid me to join her.

"How are things?" I ask, never looking her way.

"Can we please not?" She doesn't bother to tear her eyes from the numbers.

"Not what?"

"Act like we're strangers making small talk, or worse, acquaintances." She holds her bag in front of her with both hands. Her honey hair is curled into light waves, and I allow myself to envision what it would feel like if she were mine right now. To hold her, my hand sliding to the back of her neck, under her silky soft hair, pulling her toward me.

"I'm more than willing to act like friends," I say honestly.

She quickly turns toward me with narrowed eyes. "Stop it."

The elevator dings and the doors open. I let her step in first but follow closely so she can't shove me out. It leaves us in the small space all by ourselves.

"Go to dinner with me. When I get back from Chicago." I can't help myself. I need to make things right between us.

She shakes her head, her face forward.

Something squeezes in my chest. "Imogen, let me apologize."

"It was a long time ago. Don't worry about it."

I blow out a breath. "Fine."

I know I'm accepting defeat too easily, but I also know her. I'll have to use tactics and tools only the military's most skilled tactical team knows in order for her to agree to dinner with me.

The elevator doors open, and she breezes past me.

"Aren't you joining the meeting?" I ask.

"Yes. I'll see you in there. I have to get my stuff since I was at lunch." She keeps walking down the hall and I take the opportunity to watch her go. She's always had a great ass.

"Hmm... ogling one of the employees," a woman whispers next to me.

I turn to find Jana standing there with a smirk. Her perfectly lipsticked lips are sucking on the tip of a straw that's stuck in some light-brown drink.

"I'm lost," I lie, which Jana clearly finds amusing.

She slides her arm through mine. "Let me show you to our conference room. One day, I *will* find out what went down with the two of you."

Shame washes over me like the lukewarm showers in the locker room. I say nothing, mostly because I don't like to lie if I can help it, but also because in order for her to find out, Ford or Imogen would have to open their mouths. I'm positive neither will. Scars like that aren't meant to ever fully heal, and the scar we all share sometimes still feels like an open wound.

"Nothing to tell." I shrug and feign nonchalance.

"For two people who try to act like they're indifferent to

one another, you have to agree that you make it hard to believe." Jana leads us into the conference room, flipping on the lights.

"She said there was nothing to tell?" I swallow audibly.

"I'm gonna let you in on a little secret. A lot of people don't know this about me, but I love gossip. Maybe it's a rich girl thing, I don't know. Truthfully, it's the one part of me I wish I could change, but unfortunately, once my antenna is vibrating, I want the whole story. So it's probably better that the two of you are all hush-hush." She presses a button on the phone and a woman answers. "Hi Barb, can you tell Dad I'm in the conference room with Warner Langley?"

Jana sits at the table without a pad of paper or pen. Her assessing gaze flows down my body until I feel self-conscious. Especially since she's not doing it with appreciation like most women, I think she's rating me.

"With all due respect, can you stop?" I slide into a chair across from her.

"Sorry." She laughs. "Am I making you uncomfortable?"

I nod.

"You're going to make us a lot of money. I was trying to see where we could capitalize the most. I assume you don't want to do any ads in a towel or anything?"

"I'd prefer not." I shift in my chair.

Imogen breezes into the office, avoiding all eye contact with yours truly, and sits across from me, next to Jana. She flips through her folder while Jana uses the opportunity to inspect our body language.

Luckily, Mr. Gerhardt follows close behind Imogen, and his presence in the room overtakes all the sexual tension.

"Warner!" he exclaims, pushing his big bear hand in front of me instantly.

I shake it and move to get up, but he shoos me back down.

"Imogen, nice to see you. Jana." He nods in the women's direction.

"Good afternoon, Mr. Gerhardt," Imogen says.

He claps his hands and rubs them together. "Let's get this going. I'll start just to make sure we're all clear." He swivels his chair in my direction, and I glance at Imogen, who lowers her head over the papers in front of her. Oh shit. "As you know, when you signed on, you agreed to perform certain publicity jobs for the team."

I nod.

"We want to make you the face of the Florida Fury."

"But—"

Mr. Gerhardt's hand goes up, the diamond in his gold pinkie ring reflecting the light. "It's not something we typically do here. We've always focused on guys who've been here for a while, the fan faves—banners outside, make sure all their jerseys are sold in the store and online. But we feel as though putting you out there in a prominent way might help gain some new fans. I'm not in this business to not make money, Warner."

"Understood." I glimpse at Imogen and she's still avoiding eye contact with me, focusing on Mr. Gerhardt. "With all due respect, I don't think I'm the guy who can hold up the whole team. I'm not charismatic, I'm shy in front of the camera, and I don't like to talk about myself. Maybe Ford is a better candidate."

Imogen scoffs but recovers quickly when Mr. Gerhardt glances in her direction.

"Ford is married with a daughter," he says. It grates that just because Ford's married and has a family, he can't be used as the sex symbol, so they want to take advantage of me. "You're single. You're a good-looking guy. I can't imagine you have a shortage of women rotating in and out of your bedroom."

Jana chuckles but stops when my gaze shoots to her. "I think he only wants one woman in his bed, Dad."

Thankfully, Mr. Gerhardt ignores his daughter. "Imogen and Jana have some things in mind."

He's crazy. I will not be the face of this team. "I'm sorry, but I have to decline the offer," I say before this idea gets pushed too far down the road.

Mr. Gerhardt's bushy eyebrows rise, and he glances at Jana. She produces a copy of the contract I signed, sliding it across the table, highlighted. I pull it forward and give it a quick read. Apparently my agent and my lawyer are worthless because sure as shit, it says I'm required to do whatever I can to help the team when it comes to publicity events. My jaw clenches like a vise.

I mean, I knew about the requirement, but I assumed it'd be the same as any other team—do some interviews after the games, attend a charity event or two, maybe an interview here and there for different publications.

"Now, Imogen, please go ahead and tell Warner what you've come up with." Mr. Gerhardt motions in her direction.

I push away the paper and slide out of the chair to my feet. "Like hell I'm doing this. Now I have to get ready for the game."

I walk out of the room, my heart beating a staccato rhythm. Just because I signed that contract doesn't mean I have to do what they want with a smile on my face. If I'm a complete dick, maybe they won't want me as the face of the team anyway.

CHAPTER 4

"You're going to Chicago."

Imogen

"That went about as well as expected." Jana leans back in her chair. "I'll talk to him after Chicago. Let him cool off first." She's talking to her dad, who shakes his head.

"I heard he had reservations when it came to the press, that he's a quiet guy who just wants to play the game, but that's not how it is these days. Especially with a face like his."

I should sit here and let these two handle this. After all, I'm only the hype girl. I'm not supposed to convince the hockey players to actually participate in the hype.

"He'll eventually agree, or we trade him at our first opportunity and find another hottie to take his place." Jana shrugs.

"Would serve him right. Everyone is replaceable. We all know he's not playing until he's forty. What is he? Twenty-nine?"

"Eight," Jana corrects. "I agree. He's shooting himself in the foot right now. We took him in to get his last good years."

I stop my jaw from falling open. I can't believe they talk about the hockey players like this. Like they're just a commodity and not people.

"Freeman is too green and won't be playing a ton this

season unless something happens to Drake. Burrows is probably in his last year. We just need his experience to guide the younger guys in the locker room. Drake, Petrov, and Jacobs are all on the happily ever after train. Warner's really our only option and he's a goddamn good one," Mr. Gerhardt says.

"Let me talk to him," I say without thinking it through.

Jana glances over with a cocky grin that makes me resentful for volunteering. She probably did this all on purpose.

"Why would you talking to him make a difference?" Mr. Gerhardt asks.

"You know Warner and Ford were high school buddies, Dad. Imogen is Ford's sister, so I assume she knows him a bit." With a smile, Jana swivels her chair my way. "Right?"

I nod, standing because if I don't move fast, I'll miss him. "Yeah, I'm only a year younger. Let me see what I can do, and I'll get back to you guys."

Jana continues explaining the situation to Mr. Gerhardt as though he didn't know I was Ford's sister. She sounds flustered as the door of the conference room closes. I rush to the elevator, my heels clicking on the floor.

Thankfully, Warner is sitting on the bench outside the elevator, his forearms on his thighs and his hands locked together, staring down. I've found Warner in this position many times in my life. This is him thinking, dissecting and figuring out what to do, which is a good sign. Had he not been here outside the elevator, it would've meant his mind was made up, and nothing changes Warner's mind once it's set.

My heels must alert him to my presence, and he looks up at me. His dark eyes are clouded like a thunderstorm that's waning in intensity.

I tentatively sit next to him, crossing my legs and clasping my hands in my lap. I might be hyperaware of my proximity to him, but I have to ignore the heat coming off him that feels as if it's soaking into my skin.

"They send you to talk me into it?" he says, staring ahead.

"No. I volunteered."

His head whips in my direction, eyes wide with surprise. A huff leaks out of him, and he goes back to staring straight ahead. "They have no idea what they're asking. I don't wanna be anyone's puppet. I earned this job. I've paid a shit ton of dues to get where I am, and now they want me to smile and be charismatic on television, so a few women who want to fuck me will drag their friends and husbands to watch me play?"

I inhale a deep breath. "It's part of the job."

"Bullshit!" he practically yells and cocks his head, a huge breath leaving his lips. "I'm sorry. I don't want to take it out on you. And I don't want our conversation to be this way."

"What way?"

"Me pissed off and you sitting there quietly while thinking I'm an idiot for not agreeing to their demands."

"This isn't Lauder. This isn't the Upper East Side. It's not the same situation. Yes, you earned the right to be here, but promotions and marketing are part of the job. And it will only help you."

"You and my agent want me to be like that fucking monkey playing the cymbals." He stands, presses the down button on the elevator, and panic rushes through my veins.

"That's not true. I just don't want you to lose your position here."

He turns around so fast I involuntarily lean back. His face

is etched with anger and his jaw is clenched. Warner's protective of only two things in his life: his hockey career and his family. You mess with either, and he turns into a very different person than the laid-back, affable guy he normally is. "Is that what they said? That what? They're going to release me first chance they get if I don't model in my fucking underwear?"

A woman walks by and stops, having heard Warner's outburst. I'm so new I don't know who she is, but I do know we shouldn't be having this conversation in the hallway of the executive offices.

The elevator doors open, and I push Warner inside and press the ground floor button.

"What are you doing?" he asks.

"Saving you from yourself," I mumble.

"I don't need saving. I need you all to remember that I'm a hockey player. That's what I do." He raises his hands above his head. "Fuck!" Then he shoves them in the pockets of his slacks.

His suit is charcoal and shows off his body well. I've been trying to ignore the pull in my nether regions ever since I saw him downstairs.

"Calm down. These are different times. Players come to the hockey league from all different areas of life. What happened at Lauder isn't going to happen here."

His eyes meet mine, and it's clear that all the hurt from back then is still alive inside him. People he thought were his friends turned their backs on him. Everyone but Ford, that is. Until the shit hit the fan and Ford abandoned him. Then Warner lost me too.

"That's what you think I'm worried about?" He's practically seething.

The elevator doors open, and he walks out without

waiting for me to go first. I follow, unsure of what to say. What other reason could there be?

"Warner," I say, and he stops once he's outside and circles around so fast, I step back and the tip of my heel wedges into a crack in the cement. "Shit." I fall back, but Warner grabs my arms to straighten me. "Thank you."

I slide my foot out of my heel and Warner bends down to free it from the crack. "I gotta go. I appreciate you trying to get me to do this, but I made a promise to myself that I refuse to break and..." He inhales and exhales.

His cryptic talk makes me miss the days when he told me all his hopes and dreams, his fears and insecurities. When we'd lain in the dark theater room late at night while the whole house was sleeping, and he'd confess everything to me as if I was his personal diary.

Stepping back, he doesn't turn around right away, but the minute he does, panic hits me like the lash of a whip.

"What if I promise to protect you? I can steer the narrative. We could work together on this." I close my eyes, unsure why I want to protect him. What does it matter to me? If he was gone and out of Florida, it would make my life a helluva lot easier. But there's always been that small soft spot for him in my heart.

He stops but keeps his back toward me. "You don't need to do that, Imogen."

The whip that struck me earlier comes back and slashes at my heart. Warner refusing to accept help isn't something new.

"Fine! Fine, Warner. Have it your way."

He slowly circles around and our eyes lock. I refuse to step forward, even if there's a magnetic energy between us that feels as though it's drawing us together.

A horn honking pulls both of our attention to the

entrance of the arena, and I spot Ford's Bronco speeding in. He lays on the horn again and skids to a stop. The driver's side door opens and Ford flies out, wearing his suit. "What the hell is going on here?"

"Nothing," I say.

"We're just talking," Warner says. "What? I can't even say hello to your sister?"

I tilt my head and sigh. Can't Warner lessen the attitude he gives back? We both know Ford has a reason to be protective of me when it comes to him.

"No." Ford shakes his head. "You can't. You lost that right a long fucking time ago."

Warner shakes his head. "Yeah, this is the last thing I wanna deal with today." He walks to his car and slides in, the engine roars to life, and he speeds out of the parking lot.

I'm not sure where he's going since the team has to board the plane soon.

"Why do you do this to yourself?" Ford asks once Warner's gone. "Just ignore him. He'll be gone eventually."

Ford is wrong on that account. I love Tweetie, but Warner proved himself last year. He's going to be the starting left wing. And as long as he becomes the face of the Florida Fury—which will infuriate my brother—Warner's not going anywhere.

"Jeez, I can handle myself. Leave it alone," I snipe.

"Handle it yourself? Like you did—"

I poke him in the chest. "Don't go there. It was a long time ago and I'm over it. Stop protecting me."

He holds up his hands and looks down at my finger digging into his chest. "He's just an asshole who's always trying to get ahead however he can."

I narrow my eyes at my brother. "You're lying to yourself, and we both know it."

Ford says nothing because he knows I'm right.

"I'm going back to work." I spin and head inside. The elevator car is still there, so I climb in and press the button for the top floor.

Jana is waiting for me when the doors open. She's on the reception couch, fiddling with her phone. "There you are. So?"

I shake my head.

"Well, that leaves only one option," she says.

"Which is?" I walk toward my office, and she follows.

"You're going to Chicago."

I laugh. "No, I'm not."

"Yep. My dad thinks you're the person to get him to give in to our demands."

I enter my small office and close the door behind Jana. "What does that have to do with me going to Chicago?"

"If Warner won't do it willingly, we'll do it for him. You'll take some candid pictures and post them on our socials. Warm him up to the idea of being the poster boy for the organization and let him see it's not that bad."

"Jana—"

She raises her hand. "I can't argue with my dad. We're already in five other disagreements at the moment. Just go to Chicago, snap a few photos, and we'll discuss when you get back. Hopefully by then, Warner will have come to his senses and agreed."

"Are you serious?" I cross my arms.

"Go home and pack your bag."

My head falls back so I'm staring at the ceiling. Damn it all to hell. Why do I feel as if I'm going to be forced to face the past on this little trip?

CHAPTER 5

"You should go."

— Warner

Warner

Once I'm seated on the airplane, I open my book, not in the mood to talk to anyone. As much as I like Cory and Kane, I don't feel comfortable telling them about Mr. Gerhardt asking me to be the face of the team.

A few minutes later, Cory plops into the seat next to me. "Close your eyes for a second."

"No."

"As your best friend on this team, I highly advise you to listen to me."

I shut my book. "Why the hell would I close my eyes?"

Then I hear the sound of arguing coming onto the plane and I know Cory's trying to do me a solid by not having to see that Imogen is here.

"This is stupid. Why do they want you to travel with the team? No one wants the visiting team to hype themselves up. Your position is here, in Florida," Ford says.

I watch as brother and sister argue while they walk down the aisle.

"Oh my God, can you please stop talking? I have a migraine." Imogen massages her temple.

"Here, Imogen, you can have my seat." Tweetie stands up from the seat on the other side of the aisle from me.

"Thanks, Tweetie," Imogen says, but Ford pushes her forward.

"Go to hell, Tweetie." Ford narrows his eyes at me. "If I find out that you swindled a key card for her hotel room, you're a dead man."

I hold up my hands. "Must suck to be so angry all the time."

"I'm only ever angry when you're around."

"Technically, it's when I'm around your sister." I can't help but egg him on. I've stayed clear of Imogen for almost ten years. Get over it.

Ford stops and stares at me, his jaw clenching.

"Just go." Tweetie pushes Ford, and he stumbles forward.

"We've got a fifth on the game today, boys. Imogen's gonna place with us," Ford yells toward the back of the plane.

I don't turn around to see how far Imogen ends up from me, but I do wonder why she's traveling with us. Before I can give it too much thought, the pilot gets on the speaker and asks for everyone to be seated and put on their seat belts.

I do as he says, remembering the first time I knew Imogen was too enticing to stay away from.

"Warner's staying for dinner, Bennie," Ford said when we entered his kitchen.

I was trying to act as if his penthouse bordering Central Park was just like any of my friends' houses. Like the fact that he had a doorman and now a cook and I was pretty sure I saw a maid when we first walked in, like that was all normal for me. Not.

"You need to tell me sooner. It's five minutes before mealtime."

I came out from behind Ford's back to see that the chef had a Hawaiian shirt and a scruffy beard.

"Well, you must be the new friend," Bennie said.

"I'm Warner." I gave him a small wave.

"Langley," Ford said, grabbing a piece of potato and eating it. "Langley Wines."

"Oh, the Jacobs love the Langleys."

My stomach twisted, and I froze. Lying to people at school had never been my intent, but the more people kept saying Langley Wines, the more it seemed like it would be easier to just go with it. No one in those circles would understand that I was the kid from the other side of the tracks and their prestigious school was paying my tuition in order to get me to play for their hockey team with the hopes of winning a championship. When I first showed up, I assumed they all knew. I'd prepared myself for the bullshit that would come once they knew how poor I was. But the administration kept it a secret and said I was just a transfer. I wasn't sure what their end game was.

"Bennie, I said no carbs. I can smell that bread all the way upstairs." Imogen came into the kitchen and stopped when she saw me.

Our eyes met, and I told myself to look away, but I couldn't. She was so beautiful. Definitely the most beautiful girl I'd ever seen. Shiny blond hair, sparkling blue eyes, a body that didn't have one flaw as far as I could tell. It was the first time I'd seen her out of the uniforms we wore at school, and the designer jeans and tight cropped T-shirt worked for her.

But she was Ford's sister, and he'd made it clear she was off-limits. I had to respect the only guy who'd taken me under his wing, making me one of the most popular guys in school. And I'd only been there two weeks.

"Sorry, princess, but what Daddy Warbucks wants, Daddy Warbucks gets. And fresh bread was on the menu," Bennie said.

She grunted and picked up a green bean, tilting her head back and dropping it into her mouth. I shifted my stance to hide my *growing erection, and she smiled as if she was playing some game with me. Fuck me, did she do that on purpose?*

A woman who I assumed must be Ford's mom came in. "How much longer?"

"Can everyone get off my back?" Bennie said, from where he was at the oven.

"Sorry, Bennie." She laughed and patted Ford on the back. "How was everyone's day?"

Ford shrugged. "Coach is being a prick. This is Warner. Langley. Langley Wines."

I hated that every time he introduced me, it was accompanied by a lie, but I was too chickenshit to say anything.

"Oh, the spilled wineglass logo, right?" Mrs. Jacobs put out her hand. She was night and day from my mom. Both were beautiful, but Mrs. Jacobs looked fresh and relaxed without a care in the world, while my mom always looked weathered and worn out.

Everyone's eyes were on me, so I nodded.

Her hand ran down my arm. "No need to be shy in this household. And on account of your family, I'll go grab a bottle."

She disappeared while I stood awkwardly with my hands shoved in my pockets. I felt like an outsider, watching Ford mess with his sister about her friend Cici while Bennie complained about the weather outside and questioned why he hadn't gone to Hawaii when he'd had the chance to work for another family. Mrs. Jacobs returned and opened up the wine and thankfully didn't ask me any personal questions about a family I didn't know.

Finally, what felt like a lifetime later, we each took a seat in the dining room that overlooked Manhattan. I was in awe of the view while everyone else at the table piled food on their plates, apparently having no appreciation for what they had.

"It's a great view, right?" Mr. Jacobs said from my right.

I nodded. "It is."

"Three generations have lived here now."

I'd figured Ford was old money. There was definitely a mixture of old and new money at Lauder, but old money was easy to spot. Mostly because the new money showed it off, while the old money just had the confidence and arrogance that went along with it.

"Don't bore Warner with the family business talk. Tell us, Warner, do you play hockey as well?" Mrs. Jacobs wiped her hands on a napkin in her lap.

"Yes, ma'am," I said. "Left wing."

"Actually, he plays a lot of center too," Ford mumbled around his chicken. "Crazy fast and definitely giving us a chance at the championship this year."

I felt my cheeks redden, and I glanced across the table at Imogen, who was looking down at her plate.

"That would be nice. Have you played long?" Mrs. Jacobs asked.

Mr. Jacobs picked up his phone, mumbling something about a waste of time.

"I've played as long as I can remember. I'd skate as soon as the pond froze over." I smiled at her and spooned myself a helping of the potatoes.

"Oh, how lovely that you have some acreage. It's the one thing here I miss, living with land. Do you have ducks? What about horses?"

"There are ducks," I answered, which, technically, was true. There were ducks everywhere in New York state. And the pond wasn't far from our two-bedroom apartment.

"You'll have to show me pictures sometime."

"We have a good shot of winning it all, Dad. And if we make it to the championship and win, I'm sure we're both looking at full

rides to college." Ford looked at his dad with a hopeful expression, waiting for a reaction he didn't get.

His dad frowned. "You don't need a full ride. You're not some impoverished kid. You'll go to Harvard for business, just like me." There was a finality in his voice, and at that moment, I felt horrible for Ford.

Ford lowered his head and picked his fork back up without a word.

"Do you come to the games?" I asked Mr. Jacobs.

"Someone has to work to keep this view," he said, staring out the window for a moment. "I've attended a few though."

"Two," Ford said with displeasure.

"You should see Ford now," I said, trying to help. "He amazes me how quick he is around the net. Coach has been using us on this play that's sure to beat out competition."

Imogen looked up from her plate, and our eyes caught over the two lit candlesticks. She smiled softly and glanced at Ford.

"I'll see what I can do, but I'm sure your dad told you too, Warner, there's no future in hockey. You get injured, and it's over. It's fun for you two to play now in high school, but Ford will be taking over Jacobs Enterprises. I assume there's a position for you at Langley Wines?"

"I haven't thought much about it at this point. I really love hockey." Again, I teetered on the edge of lying and my stomach felt sick because of it.

Mr. Jacobs shook his head. "Youth."

"Will you be going to the game, Imogen?" Mrs. Jacobs asked.

She was pushing her food around on her plate. "I'm not sure."

"What? You go to all the games. Why wouldn't you go?" Morgan, their little sister, chimed in.

Imogen shrugged. "Stay out of it, Morgan."

The rest of dinner was spent with Mr. Jacobs talking about business and Mrs. Jacobs trying to pull information from her kids about their lives. Ford and I discussed the line and some moves we thought would work. I'd never had a friend like Ford before. Someone who loved hockey the way I did. Mostly because the kids in my neighborhood couldn't afford to play hockey and there weren't many ice rinks around us.

Once we'd finished eating, we all got up from the table. No one helped Bennie clear the table, and it felt so weird to walk away from the mess.

Ford and I retreated to his bedroom, that was the same size as my entire apartment.

"I should probably get going soon." I'd been fortunate that our neighbor, Izzy, had been able to watch Julien and Trinity.

"Where do you live?" Ford asked, thumbing through his phone.

"Not far," I said, putting on my shoes and grabbing my jacket.

"I was thinking after the game, there's this party I got invited to. Want to go?"

I shrugged. "Sure." I wasn't really a party guy, especially around my classmates. I was afraid I'd say or do something to out myself. But it felt rude to say no.

"Awesome. See you tomorrow."

I walked out of his room and down the stairs to their elevator. I'd never get used to this life. I saw no one as I made my way to leave, and I wondered if they were lonely, living with so much space. Was my family so close because we were stuck together like sardines in our apartment?

The elevator dinged that it had arrived, and to my surprise, Imogen was standing inside with a plastic bag in her hand.

"Hey," I said, unsure what else to say. I hadn't really talked to her one on one yet, although I'd thought about it a lot.

"Hi." She raised her bag. "Morgan was going to tattle on me for being out past curfew last night, so I told her I'd get her a carton of ice cream."

"What flavor?"

"Chocolate chip."

"Good choice."

We switched spots, putting me in the elevator and her in the foyer, and a waft of her perfume hit me. I instantly fell in love with the scent, though I wasn't sophisticated enough to know what it was.

"You should go, you know." I pressed the lobby button.

"Go?" she asked and tilted her head in this adorable way.

The doors began to shut.

"To the game. Friday night. You should go."

Her mouth opened slightly as the doors slid closed.

I knew I had to get my feelings under control before I lost my only friend at Lauder, but that proved impossible.

CHAPTER 6

Imogen

As if being on a plane with no option of escaping Warner's presence isn't enough, I'm standing only two people behind him, waiting to check into the hotel. Maybe I should've told Jana everything. She surely would've understood when I told her I absolutely cannot travel with this man.

Ford comes to my side, wearing a suit and carrying the brown leather bag he uses when he's only traveling for one night. "I told Tweetie he's on his own. We'll bunk together."

I narrow my eyes at him. "I'm sorry? Bunk together?"

"Don't worry, Tweetie loves that he gets his own room. Said he wished I'd told him sooner, and he'd have invited Tedi, but whatevs. Just like old times." He puts his arm around my shoulders.

I circle out of his hold. "We've never shared a room, so it's not like old times, and I really wish you'd trust me here."

"It's not you I don't trust." His gaze drifts toward Warner.

"You need to stop this," I whisper. "It's embarrassing, and pretty soon every one of your teammates is going to know what happened."

"All they need to know is that I don't want you and him together." Ford doesn't move and I want to shove him in the shoulder like I used to.

"You're not staying in my room. I'm an adult, if you haven't noticed." I raise my voice and the teammate in front of us turns around.

"I'll take you to a nice restaurant after the game. You can have anything you want to eat."

We step forward in line. "I don't want dinner. Don't you go out with the boys after the game?"

"Not since I got married and had a kid. I mean sometimes, but they're going to some club tonight." He makes a face that shows he's not into it.

"Really?" My eyebrows shoot up and I step up to the check-in desk, giving them my name. "I think I'll go there then. I was going to call Cici anyway."

"You're not calling Cici and you're not going to the club. We're going to the best steak house in this city." He pulls out his phone.

"Take Tweetie, Ford. I'm going to the club." I pass my ID to the hotel clerk.

"How many keys do you need?" she asks.

"Two," Ford says.

"One." I hold up my finger and scowl at my brother. "He's in another room."

She hands me a key card. I thank her and turn for the elevators.

Ford seethes with frustration beside me. "You're being ridiculous. You think he can't get a key to your room?"

We step into the elevator alone. Luckily, this is a bigger hotel, so there are numerous ones. Plus, I think people sense we're fighting and who wants to get into a small space with no exit?

"He's not a serial killer. He's not even interested in me anymore. Leave it alone."

I press the button for my floor and wait for him to press

his. He doesn't because he's like a little gnat flying around my face and won't leave me alone.

"Who do you think you're kidding? You two were making out in my house. Do you think I forgot?"

I roll my eyes. "That was a mistake. I didn't have my guard up. All he wanted to do was apologize."

"And somehow you ended up sucking face with the guy."

The bell dings and I step out onto my floor. So do three hockey players from the elevator to my left.

I walk down the hall, ignoring the whispered wonder-ings as to why my brother is treating me like a fifteen-year-old who wants to be captain of the puck bunnies.

"Listen, Ford, I understand your concern, but I got this. Warner and I are nothing anymore. And seriously…" I look right and left down the hall. "I really want this job and I can't succeed if everyone thinks of me as your little sister who can't handle herself. You staying in my room would say exactly that. How will they trust me if they don't think you do?"

He blows out a breath and runs his hands down his neck, pulling as he usually does when he's stressed. "You're joking about going to the club, though, right?"

I widen my eyes and wait for him to take back his question.

He holds up both hands. "Fine. I'll step back—slightly. But I have eyes in every room. News will travel back to me. You can be sure of it."

"You do realize you're my brother, not my father, right? I don't owe you any explanations."

He steps toward my door. "In that case."

I shove him away. "Go to your room, call your wife, talk to your baby, and get ready to kick Chicago's ass."

"Deal." He kisses my forehead. "Behave, little one."

"Don't I always?"

He raises his eyebrows, swivels on his dress shoes, and heads down the hall.

ONCE I'M SETTLED in the hotel room and I know for sure that Ford is at the rink, preparing for the game, I call Cici. She moved to Chicago three years ago when she met the man of her dreams.

"What the hell? Do you have the wrong number?" Cici answers.

I laugh. "It goes both ways."

"I know. Sorry, it's been crazy. How are you? Heard you're working for the Florida Fury with Warner Langley now. Feed me all the gossip."

"Well, first of all, I'm in Chicago."

She squeals and I pull the phone away from my ear. "Drinks." She muffles the phone, but I can still hear her. "Mario, I'm going out!"

"To a hockey game," I add.

She groans. "Never mind, hun."

"Come on. I really want to see you and I have to go for... well, we can discuss when I see you. You owe me for moving away and never calling anymore."

She laughs. "Guilt-tripping me? That's how you're going to get me to agree, huh?"

"And there's the added bonus of an ice rink full of hot hockey players."

"I'm married," she says.

"So? You can be married and appreciate a good-looking man." I really don't want to go by myself, and although I told

Ford I could handle all this, I'm not sure I can. To sleep literally on the same floor as Warner will drive me crazy tonight.

"Can you get Mario a ticket?"

"Sure." I'd wanted it to just be Cici and me, but getting to know Mario a little better will be nice.

"Okay, we'll come get you. Where are you staying?"

I give her all the information and tell her I'll meet her by will call at the arena. There's no reason why she should come here first. Then I set out to look the best I can, because although I'm totally over Warner, I am female and he is my ex. He needs to see what he gave up all those years ago.

* * *

AFTER WE'VE SAID our hellos, we go inside the arena, and I lead Cici and Mario down to the first-row seats. Mario's arms are full of nachos, candy, and beer. I have a suspicion that Cici is pregnant and not telling me since she declined a drink, but I'll wait for her to feel comfortable. We slide into our seats just as Chicago announces their starting lineup.

"There's Imogen's brother." Cici points Ford out to Mario.

"Nice. He's big."

"They're all big, babe." She laughs and looks at me like *get a hold of my man.*

"Do you watch hockey?" I ask him.

"I watch soccer. The better sport."

We all laugh, and the puck gets dropped, Aiden Drake passing it to Ford. The two go back and forth until Aiden passes it to Warner, who slides around the back end of the net and taps it in. The red buzzer goes off and Warner's arms go up in the air.

We all cheer. What a great start to the game. And the

business side of me can't help but think this will help in our efforts to make him the "it" member of the Fury.

"Still the king, I see," Cici says. "I can't imagine this is easy on you."

I don't want to talk about Warner and me, I just want to enjoy the game, but it's hard to concentrate on anyone but Warner.

The game continues and Drake scores another point for the Fury, but Chicago comes back with a point in the second period. Cici explains hockey to Mario throughout, while my eyes stay trained on number thirty-four.

Warner still has that little smirk when he beats another player from the opposing team. And when he shoots and scores his second goal, he looks for me in the stands. When we were younger and no one knew about us, everyone thought he looked at his classmates in the stands, but I always felt his eyes on me.

This time it's brief, but as soon as the buzzer goes off, the first thing he does is lock eyes with me. My stomach somersaults, wishing I could give him my secret sign—licking my lips—but instead I turn away, not having the heart to see him strip his gaze from me.

"You're in so much trouble." Cici elbows me. "You still have the hots for him. I mean, I get it. I do. Look at him. He's all man now. But you have to remember what he did. It's unforgivable, Imogen."

"I know. But I can't control who I find attractive either." I take a sip of my drink.

"Can we relax on discussing how hot another man is while I'm in the vicinity?" Mario chimes in. He's no slouch. The man is gorgeous with a capital G. Dark wavy hair, olive complexion, and speaks with a delicious Spanish accent that makes anything sound romantic. Especially when he speaks Spanish in a low voice to Cici and she blushes.

"You know they don't compare to you." She squeezes her husband's thigh.

"I spend my time behind a desk. Look at these guys."

"You're the vice president of a bank." Cici thumbs at her husband and shakes her head as though he's underselling himself.

"Still, I'm pretty sure if we had to take off our shirts, they win." He points toward the ice.

I follow his direction to see Ford and Aiden in a heated discussion on the bench. Warner is talking with Cory, who looks pissed from where he sits on the bench. Before I get a chance to read anyone's lips, the starting lineup is called back on the ice and Chicago scores on the play.

The Chicago fans to my right stand and bang on the partition as Ford skates by. They're screaming and putting up their middle fingers. Ford just laughs at them and shoots the puck to Aiden, who looks annoyed to be receiving the puck. The whole line looks discombobulated.

"Remember how well Ford and Warner worked together? They were like watching a figure skating team." Cici crosses her legs. "Ford hasn't passed to Warner one time tonight."

Huh, she's right. I didn't notice until right now, but Aiden had both assists to Warner tonight. Ford needs to play nice and do what's best for the team.

Warner and Aiden do some sort of play back and forth, allowing Aiden to shoot the puck into the net, putting us ahead by two. The fans next to me go crazy, complaining that there should have been a penalty called on the play. One guy throws his beer in the air, and it lands all over my lap.

"What the hell?" I scream, standing as if that's going to do anything. I smell like a brewery.

Ford comes up to the glass. "You fucking moron!"

"Ford's getting all protective again," Cici says.

I look up, but Ford's shaking his head, about to skate off. Warner is still giving the death stare to the man who dumped his beer on me. He just stares until the whistle is called, then he skates off.

Mario stashed a pile of napkins in his back pocket, so I blot as much as I can. The jackass never even apologizes, just orders another beer.

The next time the Fury are down on our end, Warner slams one of the Blackhawks against the partition where the guy next to me is standing. His beer crumbles between the partition and his stomach, soaking him. Warner winks at me and skates off.

"Karma!" Cici yells at the guy. "Or just a guy sticking up for his girl."

"I'm not his girl," I tell her.

"Imogen, you'll always be Langley's girl."

Mario distracts her, asking her about a penalty and how long the player will be in the sin bin and why it's called that.

But I can't help but think about what Cici said and how right she is. I'm afraid Warner will always hold a piece of me, and that's why I can't allow any more lines to be crossed. We have to be professionals if either one of us will survive this.

Lord knows I almost didn't survive the fallout of us once. I know I wouldn't a second time.

CHAPTER 7

"Deal then."

Warner

I head down the hallway of the hotel with Cory, making our way to the elevator to bring us to the main level.

"Come out with us," he says for the twentieth time tonight. "Some of the puck bunnies are meeting us."

I'm not sure what's up with Cory lately. He wasn't really into the women last season, except for that girl he hooked up with at Ford's wedding, but he's working overtime in the getting laid department now.

"Nah. I'm beat. That's what happens when you get ice time." I hit him lightly in the shoulder, so he knows I'm kidding.

One day, Cory—or Jet, as he's known—will be all over the ice. He's moved up in the lines, but Drake is still too damn good. Everyone pays the price of being a rookie. God knows I did at first. I doubted myself and almost left the league because I hardly got playing time.

"Well, Tweetie's on my line now and he wants to bond." Cory fixes his watch.

The man cleans up nice. Women are already holding up signs for him and waiting for him outside the locker room. Those are good signs of him being a superstar one day, if he can keep up his performance on the ice.

"It's good to bond with the other players. God knows I'm the outcast you don't want to be associated with."

"Why does Ford have such a beef with you?"

The elevator dings and the doors slide open to the main level.

I shrug. "We went to the same high school."

"You competed for the same position?"

"Nothing like that. Nothing on the ice. It's personal."

"His sister?" Cory asks and glances at me from the corner of his eye.

I stop at the restaurant where I plan to grab something to eat. "I don't wanna talk about it, but yeah. The three of us have history."

A few of the other guys come down, all dressed similarly to Cory. Slacks and button-downs, looking like the VIPs they'll be treated as tonight.

"Freeman!" Tweetie yells across the lobby.

Cory holds up his finger at them. "You know if you ever want to talk, I'm here for you. I don't have to go out."

I gently shove him toward the guys. "Go. I'm fine."

He walks backward, his eyebrows raised in question. Cory's a great guy. Hopefully, when his time comes and his jersey is one of the most popular, fame doesn't go to his head.

"See ya, Freeman." I wave and turn toward the restaurant, only to spot Imogen sitting in the corner with her computer, alone.

I look around for any sign of Ford. He's like a hawk, constantly watching her from afar. But I understand his protectiveness. If she was my sister, I wouldn't want her with a guy like me either. Especially after all the pain I caused her. But she's not my sister and I feel the exact opposite of platonic toward her. I know I should stay away, but I can't help but be drawn to her.

"Can I help you?" the hostess asks.

"Table for one." I raise my finger.

I've grown used to the kind of smile she gives me. She thinks I'm good-looking. Probably already knows I'm a hockey player because someone told her the Florida Fury are staying here, not because she's a fan. And now that I'm here alone, she wonders if I'm the type of player who brings girls to his room late at night after a game.

She'll be disappointed in a second.

She picks up a menu and starts walking the opposite direction as Imogen.

"Actually..." I touch her arm and she doesn't pull away. Instead, she veers closer, as though I have to tell her a secret. "Could you sit me next to the blonde over there?"

Her smile vanishes like I knew it would and she turns in that direction. "Sure."

Imogen looks up as the hostess places the menu on the table next to her and takes away the extra silverware. "What are you doing?"

"Having a late dinner. The same as you." I eye her barely touched salad, but empty glass of wine.

"I mean, why are you sitting next to me?" She closes her laptop. I wonder what she was working on.

"Where's Cici? I figured you two would be going out tonight." I pick up the menu like my intent was always to dine in. I had planned to take it back to my room, but Imogen changed those plans.

"She's home with her husband. That's who we were sitting with." She packs up her computer and I figure she's going to make up an excuse to leave.

"Cici's married? That's a shocker. I thought he was some

guy she convinced to buy her everything from the concession stand."

She chuckles and my heart feels as if it has wings over the fact that I made her laugh. Once upon a time, she found amusement in everything I said. Now I'm lucky if her lips tip up.

"Mario isn't a hockey guy, so she spent most of the night explaining the game to him." She slides her salad in front of her and I can't help but be thankful she might stay.

The waitress approaches the table and I give her my order of a burger and a Coke.

"Still eating whatever you want?" Imogen asks, forking her lettuce.

"Still staying away from carbs?"

She sticks out her tongue in a playful manner. Maybe we can rekindle something between us. When the waitress asks if she needs anything else, Imogen holds up her glass. "I just drink my calories now."

"Don't drink too much. I'd hate to have to walk you back to your room tonight." I smirk and she shakes her head, but I catch her blush.

She points her fork at me. "That's why we can't work together."

"Why's that?" I ask, wanting to hear her say it.

"Because you still think your flirty ways will get me in your bed and I'm not ever going back there."

"Is that a fact?"

She shoves a mouthful of lettuce in her mouth and a drip of dressing falls down her chin. I lean over and raise my hand to catch it before it drips on her clothes, but she's quick to shake her head vehemently and draw back.

"See? You can't do that," she says.

"I can't help a friend who was about to get an oil-based salad dressing on her expensive sweater?"

"You can't help your ex, who you screwed over." She takes a napkin and wipes all around her mouth. Her hair is pulled up in a messy bun and she's still dressed in what she wore to the game—tight jeans and a fitted white sweater that looks like cashmere. "And we're not friends."

"We could be." I nod a thank you to the waitress for bringing me my Coke.

"In what lifetime? Surely not this one."

"I said I was sorry. I wish I could make it up to you, but sadly, my time machine is broken." I knock my straw on the table to remove it from the wrapper and put it in my drink, feeling her seething eyes on me the entire time.

"You're making a joke of it?"

I lower my head and want to kick myself for trying to mask the pain I caused us both. "Not at all. I just…"

"What, Warner? Want to pretend it didn't happen?" The pain in her voice is like a kick in the gut and the air rushes from my lungs.

"I just want to be around you. I swear I was the best version of myself with you in my life."

She slides her salad away from her and collects her bags. "It's just like you to want more from me."

"I don't want anything from you. I just want…"

She sits on the edge of the chair, her tote bag swung over her shoulder and her purse in her hands. "What?"

I open my mouth and blow out a breath, unsure how to word it. Anything I say will piss her off. "How much do you like this job?"

"What?" Her face twists as if she isn't following where I'm going.

"This new job with Florida Fury. Who sent you on this trip and why?"

She sulks down in her chair, but she doesn't put down the bags. "I was supposed to get candid photos of you to use, per Mr. Gerhardt, but I didn't do it. I'll be going back tomorrow and telling them they might as well fire me."

The space between my eyebrows creases. "Why didn't you? You could've gotten me on the ice, off the ice, coming off the plane."

I've seen the pictures people can get when you're not looking. It's as impressive as it is annoying.

"It felt like playing unfair. Even after everything... I couldn't do that to you." She stares at her hands twisting in her lap. I'd do about anything to hold those hands and reassure her what a great person she is.

"I'll make you a deal then."

"No deal." She stands from the chair.

"Why not?"

"Because you're going to make a deal to benefit you." She's still standing in front of me, so I have her attention.

I lean back in my chair, and the waitress appears, putting my burger down in front of me. I thank her. "Sit down and we'll discuss."

She scoffs. "I'm not sitting down until you tell me what I'd get out of this deal."

"Fair enough. You get my cooperation."

"Go on..."

"To be the face of Florida Fury. I'll do it. Interviews, photo shoots, whatever you want me to do, but it's all up to you, Imogen. Not Jana and not Gerhardt. I'll do what you think is best."

She pulls out the chair and sits on the edge, the bags still hanging over her shoulders. "I don't have control over that. I'm a newbie. Gerhardt has the team under a microscope."

"I have faith in you. You always get what you want in the end."

She looks away from me for a moment. "So, anything? Even a bachelor auction if required?"

"If you can handle seeing me woo a woman who isn't you, sure."

She huffs. "Photo shoots? So you'll pose in your underwear now?"

I chuckle. "You know you're dying for me to."

"Always so fucking arrogant. What do I have to lose in this deal? What are you gaining?" She drapes her bags on the back of the chair.

I pick up her salad from the table next to us and place it in front of her. I'm amazed that I was able to get her to stay here, let alone eating at my table.

"It's just me and you. Everything I do, you're there."

"I have to be there." Her voice is monotone.

"You want me to put another stipulation on the deal?" I take my fry and dip it in the ketchup.

She shrugs. "I just figured you'd ask for a date or something."

"Do you want me to ask for a date?" I lean in a bit.

Her face wrinkles and she's quick to shake her head. "No."

"I think you do."

This is the most fun I've had since those nights in the Jacobs' theater room with her while everyone was asleep.

A flush creeps up her neck to her cheeks, and memories flood my brain of when that flush traveled the length of her body the first time I undressed her.

"Don't pretend you know me." She stabs a piece of lettuce with her fork.

"Do I not?" I arch an eyebrow.

"Not anymore. I'm not that naive girl who thought you were her whole world." Hurt still fills her eyes.

"I know you're not. And I'm not the stupid, insecure boy who refused to confront his problems."

Our gazes remain locked.

"You're not going to cop out on me halfway through?" she asks for good reason.

"No." I put out my hand between us. "You have me any way you want me."

Her delicate hand slips into mine, and the softness of her skin against my palm feels right. "Deal then."

We shake hands, then she picks up her fork again and I pick up my burger. Right before I take a bite, I say, "Don't worry, by the end of all this, you'll accept my offer of a date. But I'm not going to force you into it."

The forkful of lettuce rests in front of her lips and I wish I could snap a picture. She might be denying it, but I know she wants that date.

CHAPTER 8

"Hopefully he'll forgive me."
—Warner

Imogen

The next afternoon, I walk into Jana's office. Her legs are stretched out, her ankles crossed on top of her desk, showing the red bottoms of her expensive black heels. The phone is to her ear, but she waves me in and laughs at whatever the person says on the other end.

"You're crazy. Paisley, just worry about your Russian love. I gotta go." She hangs up and sets her cell phone on the desk, not bothering to straighten up. "So?"

I sit in the chair on the opposite side of her desk. "He's on board."

A slow smile forms on her face. "I knew you'd do it. You're a go-getter like me." I open my mouth, but she holds up her hand. "I don't need to know any of the kinky shit you did to seal the deal."

My mouth drops open. "I did nothing."

She laughs and lets her feet fall to the floor, sliding her legs under her desk and booting up her computer. "I have a good friend who does the morning show in Miami. She wants to talk to Warner."

This is a terrible starting point. Warner hates television, but I can't tell Jana no.

"Okay."

"They want him here in three days. So, he plays

tomorrow night, and the next morning, he leaves for Miami."

I had high hopes of starting this off slow. Maybe set up a meet and greet with a kid. Warner is great with kids from the little I've seen. But I don't want her to see me having problems so quickly.

"Do you think he can handle this himself? He's not going to be a no-show or anything?" she asks as she types on her computer.

"Well... that's the thing."

Her fingers stop punching the keys and she rests her forearms on the arms of the chair, linking her hands together. "What?"

"In order for him to agree to be the face of the team, I had to agree to accompany him to everything he has to do."

She laughs, her head falling back to the headrest of the chair. "Man, I like this guy."

I roll my eyes.

"Come on. He knows how to get what he wants."

I cannot let my boss think I'm trading sexual favors for Warner's cooperation. "That's not it. I think he just trusts me to steer the narrative for him."

"Exactly. He *trusts* you. And most of the time, when a man trusts a woman he isn't biologically related to, it means he's in love with her."

Where does she get this stuff? I wave her off. "He's not in love with me. We've just known one another for a long time."

"So you're still playing the whole zipped lips game? Okay, I'll book you on the same flight. Two hotel rooms or one?"

I stare at her blankly. "Two."

"Hopefully there's not a shortage of rooms this short of

notice." She laughs and types on her computer again. "Also, my dad wants to set up an event featuring all three of the new guys. So I was thinking a meet and greet or maybe a charity event?"

"Just to clarify, we're talking about Langley, Freeman, and Burrows?"

"Of course. Although, it's kind of weird to think of them all as new when you consider where they are in their careers. Burrows's is about over, Freeman is just getting started, and Langley is in the midlife crisis zone."

I tilt my head in question.

"I know you've been around hockey your entire life because of your brother, but I've been around professional athletes a long time. When they get a number of years under their belt, they start looking at what their future holds. What's going to be there when their career is over. How old is Warner? Twenty-eight? And he never went to college, right?"

I nod.

"This is when the players usually start getting married and popping out kids. The fun years of the travel are over. The puck bunnies aren't doing it for them anymore. They've realized they're not invincible and that their career could be over at any time with a bad injury. Look at your brother."

I consider it for a moment. Until right now, I thought Lena just blew into his life unexpectedly and he fell head over heels in love with her, but was he just ready to settle down because of the stage of life he's in?

"Ford loves Lena."

"I never said he didn't. But if they'd met five years earlier, do you think they'd be married right now?" She tilts her head and looks at me.

"Probably not," I admit grudgingly.

"We need to take advantage of however many more single days we can get from Warner Langley." She picks up a piece of paper with his face on it. "He's gorgeous, a hockey star, and single."

Granted, we're not best friends, but I've never heard Jana be so cynical. "I get it."

"I'm not trying to throw a grenade in your lap. I see the way you look at Warner."

I stand to end this conversation. "I don't look at him any way except with disdain."

"Try looking in the mirror next time." She raises both eyebrows. "I'll have your itinerary sent to you once it's finalized. Don't let them talk too much about his personal life, keep it a bit of a mystery, but find an angle that will make people root for him."

As I leave Jana's office, a list of things runs through my head. Warner's life story would pull on people's heartstrings, but he'll never agree to tell the entire truth. He always gives the same answer when people ask how he started hockey. His mom gave him gear for Christmas because her boss offered it to her for free. The first time he put on all the pads and skates, he fell in love with the game. No one pries about where he grew up, and he's always quick to steer the conversation away from his family.

It's probably safest to steer clear of that time in his life because I do not want anything to come out about what happened between us. Still, as I walk into my office, I reminisce about the other night at the hotel restaurant. The way he walked me to my room after we finished eating. I wanted to invite him in but managed to stay strong. Still, the man has had the passcode to my heart from day one and I can't help but wonder how long I'll be able to keep him locked out.

Months had gone by since Warner had come to Lauder. He and Ford had become fast friends. Mostly because they had so much in common. They were on the same hockey line and tied with the same number of points because of the way they could always predict where the other one was going to skate.

Warner had been on vacation with us and spent weeknights at our house, and I spent my time daydreaming about what it might be like if he were my boyfriend. Rarely did Warner attend parties with us though. He always had an excuse, saying he had a big extended family and his parents felt family took precedence.

But that night was different. One of the girls from their grade, April, was having a party and Warner had agreed to come. Rumor was he liked April, and I tried to deny to Cici how much that crushed me. Over the months, I'd fallen for Warner, and a small part of me thought maybe he felt the same. We'd exchange looks across the table and he'd always ask about me. As his friendship with Ford developed and he spent more time with our family, Ford eased up on the whole "leave my sister alone" thing. So many times, the three of us would gossip about the happenings at school in the kitchen with Bennie.

I hadn't planned to go to April's party, but I'd complained to my mom that Ford didn't want me there and she was going to bat for me.

"Why can't you take your sister and Cici?" Mom came out of the kitchen with a bowl of popcorn. She and Morgan were binge-watching Twilight *tonight.*

"Because they're juniors." Ford put on his coat.

"Come on," I whined.

Warner was pretending there was something important on his phone. "Let's just take them. What's the big deal?" Warner mumbled, never looking right at my brother.

Ford looked at my mom and she gave him a look that made

him agree. "Fine. But when I say we're leaving, we're leaving, you got me?"

"Yep. Can we pick up Cici on the way?" She was only a block down, so there was no reason the taxi couldn't stop.

Ford groaned. "Fine."

The four of us took a taxi to April's penthouse, which wasn't as nice as ours, though it was in a new construction high-rise. That shouldn't even have been a thought at the time, but I'd been conditioned otherwise by my upbringing. Riding the elevator up, Ford razzed Warner about April.

"So do you like her?" Cici asked, her gaze slipping over to me.

"I barely know her," Warner said and shrugged.

"Well, you've got your pick. I heard everyone will be here." Ford squeezed Warner's shoulder. "Plus, you never come out on the weekend, so the chicks are going to take full advantage."

I pretended my stomach wasn't sour from listening to Ford talk about how many girls wanted Warner, and when the elevator doors opened, I weaved through them to get out first. Cici caught up to me, and we were quickly swallowed up by all the kids in our grade.

I lost track of Ford and Warner for the majority of the night until most of the party ended up in the media room. One of the hockey players, Brandon, had an empty wine bottle on the floor. Warner was in the circle on the opposite side of April, and my heart felt heavy.

"What a childish game," I murmured to Cici.

"What was that, Imogen?" Mia, one of April's friends, called, having heard me.

Mia was a pot stirrer, looking to start trouble whenever she could. She was the one who kept telling me about April and Warner. Everyone knew Warner hung out at our house a lot and always asked if I'd slept with him already. Or they asked if I'd walked in on him in the shower or if we sneaked out together after Ford went to sleep. It was all stupid rumor, no matter if I wished it was true.

"I say Imogen joins the circle," Mia said with a Cheshire grin.

"No thanks," I said in my most disgusted voice.

"Hell no. I'm not kissing my sister." Then I noticed Ford was in the circle too. Probably to arrange it so if Warner spun the bottle, it ended up facing April. Those games were always fixed.

"Imogen, come join us." Mia waved me over. "We'll call it an exception if the siblings land on one another."

"Exception if the bottle lands on anyone with my sister," Ford said.

Mia shook her head and kept her hand outstretched as though she were welcoming me in good faith, but I knew better.

"Go." Cici nudged me. Once I stepped forward a bit, everyone was pushing me over.

"I don't get you, Ford. You can screw whoever you want, but your sister can't get any action?" Mia asked and laughed.

"And here I thought you were a ditzy cheerleader," Ford said.

"Sit." Mia shoved me on the floor and my knee touched Warner's. He quickly scooted an inch away. "Now where were we? April, your turn to spin."

April shyly leaned forward, concentrating as she spun the bottle, then went back to sit on her ass.

"Change of game!" Mia yelled before the bottle stopped spinning. "Seven minutes in heaven with whoever it lands on."

My stomach rolled, and I watched the tip of the bottle slow by Warner. It was going to land on him, and I'd lose my dinner right there, watching him take April to the closet.

But the bottle slowed by Warner and inched past me, landing on Trey next to me.

I could have sworn I heard Warner blow out a breath, but I thought maybe he was upset about April having to go with Trey.

Mia didn't let up, demanding the two go into the closet in the *front room. April glanced over her shoulder at Warner, who was fiddling with his shoelaces.*

I moved to stand, ready to disappear back into the crowd, but Mia shoved me back down. "Now for our second couple."

"Let's go." Ford pushed himself up from the floor.

"You go because you can't end up in a closet with your sister. It's your turn, Imogen." Mia took my hand and placed it on the bottle.

I quickly did the math. There were three boys, all hockey players, and two girls left. The chances of the bottle landing on Warner were not on my side. I wasn't sure it mattered anyway, because there was no chance Ford would let me go into a closet with anyone.

"Someone go keep Ford busy." Mia shooed him away, and two of her friends took him by the arms and escorted him to the balcony. "Go ahead."

I was ashamed that I allowed her to pressure me into it, but I spun the bottle, and with my breath held, I watched it turn. At first it was rushing by everyone but slowed on the fourth go-around. I got dizzy from my eyes following it, but when I thought it would land on me—which would be fitting, though I'd probably be made fun of for it—it stopped on Warner.

"Thatta girl!" Cici shouted.

Warner and I shared a look.

I'd thought Ford was distracted, but he showed up out of nowhere. "Nope. Game over, Mia."

"Rules are rules, Jacobs," Mia purred.

If there was a couple I thought was meant for one another at Lauder, it was Mia and my brother. They both ruled their friend groups.

Warner put his hand on Ford's shoulder. "Better me than someone else. Don't worry."

Just like that, Ford relaxed and nodded, agreeing with his best friend. It also meant the signs I'd thought I saw from Warner were my imagination. He wasn't interested in me.

"Go, you two." Mia shooed us away just as she had April and Trey, and we went into the kitchen pantry.

The room was dark, but I heard everything going on outside. I could also smell Warner's cologne and feel the heat radiate off his body onto mine. It made me want to take shallow breaths.

"Sorry," I said.

"For what?" Warner leaned on the cabinet since it was a walk-in pantry with more space than ours at home. Bennie would be jealous.

"You should be with April," I said in a small voice.

He turned on his phone's flashlight to illuminate the space. "I'm right where I want to be, Imogen."

I felt as if a walnut was in my throat. "What does that mean?" I couldn't help asking.

He drew in a long breath before he spoke again. "Can I ask you a question?"

"Yeah?" I asked.

"Am I alone in this?"

I looked up to see his dark eyes studying my face. "In what?"

He broke the distance, and I sucked in a breath. "I'm about to be the worst friend." His palm slid along my cheek and his fingers weaved through my blond hair. "Hopefully he'll forgive me." He bent down and his lips landed on mine.

Nothing was the same after that.

I'd kissed boys before, but I'd never felt as though my feet were floating. A magical sensation ran through my body and all I wanted was more of him. More of whatever he'd offer.

CHAPTER 9

"Well, we disagree on that."
Warner

Warner

*I*t only took one day for Imogen to email me with the promo she wanted me to do. An interview with a morning show in Miami. Now, I'm sitting at the gate in the airport terminal, waiting for her to join me. We're flying down tonight because we have to be at the studio at five in the morning tomorrow.

My phone rings, and when I see it's my mom, I debate whether I want to answer it, but I slide my thumb over the screen. We barely catch up with one another these days.

"Hey, Mom," I answer.

"Great game the other night. You're making a name for yourself down there."

"Yeah, I've had some luck come my way."

She sounds impressed, but I still feel disconnected from Ford, and the more Drake works with me on the ice, the angrier Ford seems to become. Eventually, it'll come to a head on the ice or he'll have to forgive me for what I did. As unforgivable as it is. We can't go on like this.

"Warner, you know it's not luck."

"Well, you're my mom. You're supposed to think I'm the best."

She laughs. "Julien is telling everyone at school that

you're his brother. Most of his friends don't follow hockey, but one of the dads was impressed."

I bought my mom a small condo in the city after I'd been in the league for two years. We decided she wouldn't follow me because, as she put it, I had to have my own life and it was bad enough she was allowing me to buy her a condo. But I've always thought of taking care of my mom and my siblings as my job. I'm the oldest, and it's not my younger siblings' fault that their fathers didn't step up and take care of their families.

"Next time I'm in town, I'll pick him up from school."

"He'd love that. So, what are you doing today?"

I glance around the hustle of the terminal. "I'm actually headed to Miami. I have to do a morning show in Miami tomorrow. I'm at the airport now."

I purposely leave out the fact that Imogen is coming along because my mom knows our history. Of course she understands my side because she's my mom, but she also thinks Imogen and I should be able to move forward after all these years. She's a dreamer, which is why after so many men have screwed her over, she still believes her one true love is out there somewhere.

"You're doing a talk show?" Her surprise is evident in her voice.

I blow out a breath. "Yeah. Stupid really, but the owner of Fury wants me to be the face of the team, so here I am."

"Well, it is a gorgeous face. Still have those dimples women love."

I shake my head and sip my soft drink. It's crazy, but I swear I feel Imogen. I look up and sure enough, she's walking down the terminal wheeling a small carry-on behind her, a fancy coffee drink in her hand, her plump pink lips wrapped around the straw as her eyes scour the area for our gate.

"Hey, Mom, I gotta go. I'll call you in a few days, okay?"

"Be careful. Love you."

"Love you." I hang up as Imogen walks over to me and sits on the bench of seats across from me. "You made it." She looks at my phone as if she overheard me.

"Mom." I wave the phone.

"Oh, how is she?" She leans back and crosses her legs. She's in jeans and a T-shirt that says #IDontCare with an open light sweater over it. I did always love her style. Never uptight like most of the girls at Lauder.

"She's good."

"Is she in Florida now?"

I shake my head. "Still New York. Bought her a place in Brooklyn."

She smiles. "Best son ever."

"Her expectations aren't high." I sip my soft drink.

"It's really nice, Warner. But I'm not surprised." She picks up her drink and looks at the flight board. We should be boarding soon, and I wonder if we're seated next to one another, since I have no idea who made the arrangements.

"Because I'm a mama's boy?"

She shakes her head. "No, because you love your mom and your siblings. They were always your first priority."

I can't help but feel like that was a dig. A dig about the decision I made back in the day. "Imogen…"

She puts her hand in the air, shaking her head. "I didn't mean it like that."

I slide to the edge of my seat to get as close to her as I can. "I really want to talk about it."

She scoots back in her chair and uncrosses and recrosses her legs. "I don't. It's in the past, let's just leave it there."

"But—"

She shakes her head. "No, I can't."

Seeing that she's not ready to go there, I nod and slide back so my back hits the seat. Luckily, we're only sitting there for a little bit before they announce our boarding.

I have no idea who has my back at Florida Fury, but we're both in first class and I can't strip the grin off my face when I discover we're sitting next to one another.

"Should I get a blanket like old times?" I ask, putting our carry-ons in the upper compartment.

She wraps the seat belt across her waist, rolling her eyes.

"I'm just trying to lighten the mood."

I sit next to her and buckle in, not regretting my joke. We have to overcome this barrier between us if we're ever going to move forward. But clearly her mind is still occupied with memories of our demise.

———

THE NEXT MORNING, I'm second-guessing this situation I've put us in. Imogen declined my offer of dinner, saying she had a headache. She said no to picking up coffee on the way in. So here we are, arriving at the studio at the crack of dawn and barely talking to one another.

We're greeted by a guy named Ollie, the assistant to an assistant of some kind. Those are his words, not mine. Ollie shows us to the dressing room we'll be in until we go on air. He gives me the lowdown on the schedule, and as he leaves, Imogen follows him, asking to speak to him in private.

A makeup person comes in and puts way too much shit on my face as another woman comes in to do my hair. They're both friendly, but I keep wondering what Imogen is doing until she returns to the room.

"What was that about?" I ask when she sits down on the couch and boots up her computer.

"Just passing along the questions that aren't to be asked." She never looks up from her computer screen.

I stare at her through the reflection of the mirror. "What are you telling them not to ask me about?"

She looks at the hair and makeup people. "We'll talk about that later, but you trust me, right?"

I shrug. "Yeah."

"Are you guys a couple?" the makeup artist, who's hardly wearing a stitch of makeup herself, asks.

"You're definitely giving off that vibe. If you want us to leave, just say so," the hairstylist says, looking at the makeup artist. They've obviously been in awkward situations before.

"No, we're not a couple," Imogen answers for us.

"Yet," I add.

"Warner." Imogen's eyes meet mine through the mirror and she quickly shakes her head once.

"Truth is, I want to date her, but she's blowing me off."

"Are we really playing this game?" she asks me.

Both women collect their stuff.

"You're our easy one, already came in here gorgeous," the makeup artist says as they leave.

Imogen stands huffing. "What if they tell someone what you said?"

"Tell someone what? Who cares?"

"Because, Warner, there are a few things we should be clear about when it comes to you being the face of the organization. There's a reason we're not using Aiden or Ford or Maksim. They're all taken. One of the biggest things you have that they don't is that you're single." She puts her hands on her hips. She's wearing another one of those power pantsuits with a silk tank top underneath. And her heels. Every damn time I see her in heels, I imagine them digging into my ass as I fuck her.

"Just because I'm not in a relationship doesn't mean I'm single."

Her face twists in annoyance. "I don't even want to know what that means."

I stand from the chair and walk toward her. "Think about it."

The door opens and in walks the two hosts of the show, Maggie and Mitch. I wonder if those are even their real names.

"Hey, you two," Maggie says. She's a petite brunette and has that look women get when they've spent too much time under the knife and needle of a plastic surgeon.

I shake her hand, then reach out to Mitch, who is more concerned with whatever is on his phone than us. Must not be a hockey fan.

Maggie looks at Mitch in annoyance. "We just wanted to pop in and say hello. I'm sure Ollie went over everything with you. Should be quick and painless." She winks.

"Did you get the topics that are off-limits?" Imogen asks.

Maggie nods. "We did."

"Actually, nothing is off-limits. Ask me whatever you want."

Imogen huffs and her eyes burn a hole in the side of my face. "Warner," she says sweetly, but I know the syrupy sweet tone in her voice is anything but authentic.

"It's fine. They want honesty and I'll give it to them."

Maggie's smile brightens and even Mitch tucks away his phone to pay attention to the conversation now.

"That's great to hear. We do love when guests will be candid," Maggie says.

"We'll see you out there," Mitch says, shaking my hand again, never bothering to introduce himself to Imogen.

After the door shuts, Imogen walks over to her computer to pack up her stuff. "Why would you do that?"

"Because I don't want to live behind lies anymore. Because I'm damn proud of who I am and where I came from. Did you tell them not to ask me about my childhood?"

She swings her laptop bag over her shoulder. "I told them only to talk about the trade. To keep it on Florida Fury, but to not ask about... Ford."

I chuckle. "And they agreed to that?"

"They did."

"Half the league is watching how Ford and I play together, waiting for a fight to break out between us in the middle of a game."

"Warner, they're going to ask what happened between you two." Her voice is grave.

"Which is fine."

"No, it's not." Her eyes narrow.

There's a knock and Ollie peeks in his head. "We're ready for you."

I nod. "Let's go."

"Warner!"

I leave because Imogen's crazy if she thinks I'd tell them anything that would compromise her, but I'll still be as truthful as I can. Her heels click behind us on the way to the studio. They set me up with a microphone, and the entire time, Imogen is mouthing things to me. I shake my head. I've got this handled.

Once they're back on air, Maggie and Mitch introduce me, and I answer their questions as truthfully as I can. How I was surprised by my trade to the Fury and what it's been like since I joined the team at the end of last year.

It's Mitch who says, "It's no secret that you and Ford Jacobs aren't friends. There were a lot of fights on the ice between you guys when you were on opposing teams. Now you're teammates. How do you see that playing out?"

I glance at Imogen. She walks toward someone who looks as though they might be in charge. Probably trying to stop this before I can say anything.

"Ford and I attended the same high school. We were best friends when we played at Lauder together and got our team to the finals."

"Oh, I didn't know you were best friends in high school." Maggie plays the ditzy part she does on the show. "Did a girl come between you?" She waggles her eyebrows.

"All I will say is that some bad choices were made on my part. Choices I regret every day. Decisions I wish I could do over. I never thought I'd have the opportunity to play with Ford again or be in his life. But I believe in fate. There's a reason I was traded to his team. A reason we're playing together, and I hope I can earn back some of the friendship we once had." My gaze focuses on Imogen, who's watching intently behind the camera.

Maggie laughs. "You talk about Ford as if he's a lost love."

I shrug. "Ford had my back when not a lot of people did. Sadly, I wasn't the friend I should've been in return."

"Well, there you have it. I wasn't expecting so much honesty this early in the morning." Mitch chuckles. "Head to a Florida Fury game to see firsthand whether this friendship can be patched up. I think everyone would agree that if you and Ford Jacobs get on the same page, you've got a good shot at the Cup."

The red light on the camera clicks off and I stand and shake their hands.

Ollie escorts me back to the greenroom. I hear Imogen's heels clicking behind us as she huffs the entire way.

Once Ollie has left the room, Imogen finally speaks. "What the hell was that? This was supposed to be a fluff piece."

I whip around and she steps back, so her back is against the wall. I cage her in with an arm over her head. "Exchange every damn word I said about Ford with your name. I'm not being shy about this, Imogen. I want you back in my life. And if you won't allow us to have the conversation we need to have, then this is what'll continue to happen."

Her chest rises and falls, her breath coming in short pants. "There's no future for us."

"Well, we disagree on that." I step forward and watch her breath stagger. Sliding out my tongue, I lick my lips and stare at her for a second before pushing back off the wall.

I just want to make sure I still get to her. She wants me. Maybe it is just physical right now, but I'll push past that eventually. I'll prove to her that she can trust me with her heart, even if she couldn't the first time around.

CHAPTER 10

Imogen

"**W**hat an asshole!" Ford yells.

"Quiet down," Lena says, holding up the baby monitor.

"Why would he go on TV and say all that shit?"

I can't tell Ford that it was meant for me and not him. Although I think what Warner said probably applies to us both. I believe he wants to repair his relationship with my brother as well.

"Because he wants you guys to be friends again." Lena places a bowl of chips and salsa on the table.

We're on the back patio next to their pool. Ford called this morning, demanding I come over. Big brothers can be extremely annoying at times, even if they have your best intentions in mind. It's pretty warm out, which still feels so weird to me. Back in New York, I'd be wearing a jacket and quite possibly a hat and mittens.

"There are things in this world you can't come back from and what he did is one of them." He glances in my direction, then picks up a chip and dips it aggressively in the salsa before chomping down on it.

"Is that true?" Lena asks.

Ford stares at her and says nothing, as though she

should heed the look as a warning, but we both know Lena doesn't care about his silent brooding or loud outbursts.

"Everyone deserves a second chance." She dips her chip and eats it, smiling at me.

Why is she smiling at me? I'm in agreement with Ford. There's no second chance happening between Warner and me.

"Not him. Not ever." Ford takes another chip just as Annabelle cries. He stands. "Fuck, I'll get her."

"I can—"

He waves Lena off. "No, I need our daughter before I lose my cool and end up driving over to that fucker's house."

Ford disappears inside and Lena sets her gaze on me.

"What?" I shift in my seat.

Since Lena worked for our family before she and Ford got together and got married, I've developed a good friendship with her. Although I didn't tell her what happened with Warner until he got traded to the Fury, I've trusted her with a lot of other things.

"Tell me."

I crinkle my eyes. "Tell you what?"

"Well, I know what happened to tear you and Warner apart, but he's fighting so hard to get you back. I have to think you had a tremendous love story. How did it begin between you two?"

I bring my knees up to my chest and rest my chin on them, wrapping my arms around my legs. "Honestly?"

She nods. "Always."

"I think it was what a lot of girls dream about when they're teenagers. Warner was the most popular guy at school, and he wanted me. Plus, we kept it from Ford, so it felt like it was out of a movie."

The sound of Ford arguing with Annabelle about swimming sounds through the monitor.

"Tell me."

I shake my head. "Ford doesn't want to hear it."

"He'll be up there forever. First, they'll argue about swimming and Annabelle will get her way, then they'll argue about the swimsuit. And then he has to change her. We have time."

A smile forms on my face when I remember the kiss in the pantry at April Carrington's party. "He kissed me the first time at a party during a game of seven minutes in heaven."

"Ford let that happen?" Her eyes are wide, obviously surprised.

My smile dims. Warner played the best friend card with Ford, but the yearning between us was so strong, it was like neither of us had a choice. I didn't want to be the reason their friendship ended, and we both knew Ford wouldn't understand. He'd been so adamant about us not getting involved. I never even asked why.

"Warner told Ford he could trust him."

Lena's eyebrows rise and she takes another chip.

I sigh. "You really want to know the whole thing?"

She nods while chewing.

"After he kissed me at the party, I thought for sure that was it. That he'd either ignore me or tell me it was a mistake. But one night he stayed over after a late game, and he texted me after Ford went to bed."

Lena slides back in her chair and places her hand over her heart. "Go on."

My memory floats back to that night and the other nights afterward. When it all felt perfect.

He asked me to meet him in the theater room, so I sneaked

down there. The penthouse was dark and quiet, and we both knew that after a game, Ford crashed hard.

I reached the theater first and sat on a recliner. It was dark except for the star ceiling above me, and I snuggled under a blanket since I was wearing my pajamas.

The door opened and in walked Warner in a pair of sweats and a T-shirt, barefoot. He didn't say anything but sat in the recliner next to me. Both of us stared at the sparkling white lights in the ceiling.

"So... what's up?" I asked, whispering, although the room was soundproof. No one would hear us, but I was so nervous. My stomach was in knots.

"I just wanted to see you." He turned in his recliner to face me, and I mimicked his movements.

His hand slid under the blanket to find mine and my breath hitched with the contact. "Why?"

"Because I like you. I thought I made that clear."

"Until you ignored me for a week." I couldn't keep the hurt from my voice.

He pushed a hand through his thick, dark locks. "I kind of freaked out after I kissed you. I thought for sure Ford saw through me. That he knew I betrayed him. Then I hated myself for betraying him. He's been a great friend to me and I'm going behind his back..." He rambled on and on about how guilty he felt, but then he said the words I've never forgotten. "But, Gen, whatever this is is way too powerful for me to ignore. I can't help but be pulled to you. You're all I think about and it's making me crazy. All I do at night is lie in bed and think about hearing your voice. When you laugh, my heart catapults out of my chest. The selfish part of me wants your laughter to be because of something I said. I think about putting my hands in your hair and feeling your soft skin again."

"But—"

He put his finger to my lips. "Just tell me if you feel it too, because I'm done second-guessing myself. I do a lot of shit for a lot of people in my life, leaving myself for last. I want you, and I'm willing to step through the fire to have you."

Lena's mouth hangs open, and a strangled sound escapes her. She gets it.

"After that, we dated in secret. He would text me all the time, give me signs when he was on the ice. And we'd sneak into that theater room every time he spent the night."

"Why didn't you just tell Ford?"

"You know Ford." I shrug.

She nods, understanding how stubborn and difficult her husband can be. "But it had to be hard."

"At first there was a thrill about just the two of us knowing what we meant to each other. Then after a while, it felt like he was keeping me a secret. I'd see girls flirt with him, or Ford would say, 'So and so likes Warner and we're going on a double date.' I'd be strangled with jealousy. But he never went. Always found an excuse. Hell, I think there was a rumor that he was gay for a little while because no one understood why he didn't date any of the girls at our school when they all wanted him. I was in love with him. Still, I worried that I was just someone to pass the time with. But then, after a few months, he finally trusted me enough to confess something."

Lena's head tilts. She knows what happened between Warner and me, but I don't think she knows this part.

"We'd talked about having sex, though Warner was always patient with me." I stop for a moment and inhale. "Everyone thought his family was Langley Wines. That his parents spent a lot of time in California, and since he was a senior, he was left alone and that was the reason that he spent so much time at our place. But that night, we took the blankets and laid them out in front of the giant screen we never watched, and he told me the truth about this family."

"Which was?"

I allow myself to transport back to that moment. To feel that feeling all over again.

His knuckles brushed along my cheek. "I have to tell you something and I don't want you to be mad."

My eyes popped open, and I stared at him, my body growing stiff and tight, expecting the worst.

"I'm not Langley from Langley Wines."

"What?" I whispered, because in honesty, all my dreams of us in the future involved a lifestyle like I grew up in. One that he would be able to afford if he was the heir to Langley Wines.

"I go to Lauder on a scholarship to play hockey. I mean, I have good enough grades too, but they wanted me for the team." He moved his hand off me, and I was unsure if he thought I was going to bolt or no longer wanted him to touch me.

"So, where are you from?" My forehead wrinkled.

He sat up and brought his legs up, allowing his head to hang between them. "A part of the city you've never been to. My mom is a single mom."

"But why didn't you say anything?"

He shrugged. "Someone assumed it and more people believed it. I just went along with it because it was easier than admitting the truth."

"Which is?"

He glanced back at me, still on the floor. "That I come from nothing. That I don't have one percent of the money your family does."

I sat up and placed my hands on his arms and my cheek on his back. "It doesn't matter where you come from. Look where you're going. You're already being talked about being drafted, and if that doesn't happen, I bet you could get a scholarship like Ford will."

He laughed. "The draft is the only option for me. I can't go to college and have a job that would allow me to send money home. I need to get drafted so I can start supporting my family."

"Warner?"

His hands gripped mine. "What?"

"Why are you trusting me with this? We both know if I slip up or if something bad happens between us, people would have a field day with this information. I'd like to say it wouldn't matter, but to some, it would."

I wasn't naive about the people I grew up around. They were judgmental assholes.

"Because I want you to know me." He turned around so fast I fell to my back. He leaned over to me. "Because I love you, Gen, and I want you to love the person I really am. Not the Langley Wines lie, but me, Warner Langley. The kid on a scholarship who comes from nothing. But I promise you, I will make it. I won't be the kid with nothing for long. I'm going to work my ass off to give you everything you deserve."

I placed my hands on either side of his head. How had we fallen so fast and so deep in this short amount of time? But we had and there was no denying it. We'd already been taking chances we shouldn't. It was time to tell Ford and others.

"You owe me nothing. And I might not know your mom or how much money your family has, but I know you, Warner Langley." My one hand fell over his heart. "I know you. I'm sure of it."

And I was. At least until he had to make a tough choice. Then it felt as if I didn't know him at all.

I look at Lena and see her wiping tears from her face. Meanwhile, I'm wondering if I'll ever get over this guy.

Because talking about this has churned up feelings I'd rather stay dormant.

Ford comes out of the house with Annabelle, who's wearing her strawberry swimsuit. "What the hell happened? Why are you crying?" he asks his wife.

Lena quickly wipes under her eyes. "Nothing. Just girl talk. Here, I'll take her in."

Ford stares at Lena. "In that? I'm already in my board shorts, I'll take her. You sure you're okay?"

Lena nods and he gives her a look like we'll be talking about this later, then he walks with Annabelle into the water.

My phone dings on the table. I pick it up, surprised to see the text I do.

Warner: *I heard you want to follow me for a day. Meet at my place, six am.*

I hammer a text back to him.

Me: *Nothing happens at 6am.*

Warner: *I'm up at 6 and more than awake, so a lot happens at 6. But I go to work out so if you want to follow me around, I suggest you're here before I leave.*

I groan, and Lena tries to lean over to see.

"He's so annoying," I say in a quiet voice.

"I'm sorry, but now I kind of want him to win you over. You shouldn't have told me that story." She picks up a chip, dunks it in the salsa, and shoves it in her mouth. "I'm horrible."

"There's no coming back from where things ended with us."

If only I believed that.

"Nothing's impossible. Look at your brother and me."

I chuckle and type out a response on my phone.

Me: *Fine, I'll be there but make sure the small part of yourself that's up is all tucked away.*

Warner: *Come on. I'm sure you remember, there's no small part of me.*

I toss my phone on the table and refrain from screaming. I'm hopeless. I can't even stop myself from flirting with him by text.

CHAPTER 11

"Breakfast?"

Warner

$\mathcal{A}$t six o'clock in the morning, the camera crew knocks on my door. Imogen's not here yet, but I'm not surprised. She's never been a morning person. I let them in and finish packing my bag for the gym.

Roger, the guy in charge, goes over the agenda. We discuss my plans to go to the gym, breakfast, then off to a photo shoot for my number one sponsor, a watch company who mostly has me in print ads, though there's talk about doing a commercial for the Super Bowl this year. I haven't heard anything official from my agent yet though.

The doorbell rings and I open the door to find Imogen completely done up from head to toe. Her long hair hangs in ringlets, her makeup is on point, and she's wearing another pantsuit with heels that makes my dick ache.

"Good morning," I say with a smile.

"Uh-huh." She walks past me into the house.

I handle the introductions and grab my bag, heading out the door. "Imogen and I will meet you at the address I put on the itinerary."

"I'll follow. I can drive myself." Imogen smiles politely at Roger.

"That's ridiculous. We're all going to the same place." I nod toward my SUV.

She stares longingly toward her Mercedes. Roger goes to his van, knowing he has no other option if he wants to bring his crew and gear, which leaves us in the driveway.

"I swear you do these things on purpose," she says and stomps over to my car, shooing me away when I try to open the car door for her.

Once she's settled inside, I round the front of the SUV and climb in. It's not the newest SUV on the market, but it's no beater either. It's probably not up to the standards she's used to, but I kind of like that. I want to see if the woman I love has changed at all.

She secures her seat belt and I pull out of the driveway.

"So you really get up this early every morning?" she asks.

"Did you forget that easily?" Back in high school, I worked out every morning before school and after too. I put in double the workouts that my teammates did to ensure I'd be the best conditioned on the ice.

"I remember. Ford was always talking shit about your workouts. You trying to show up everyone else." She laughs to herself.

It's hard to keep from bringing up everything we need to discuss, but this isn't the time or place, even if I wish it were.

For the rest of the drive, she looks out the window or types on her phone. What I wouldn't have done to take her on a real date back in high school. As I glance at her next to me in the passenger seat, I can't help but remember a time when I was almost able to give her the future she deserved.

"You're entering the draft?" Imogen stared across the Jacobs' dinner table at me, excitement in her eyes.

I had been spending more time there than usual. My mom's recent unemployment meant she could be home with Trinity and Julien more than usual. She was actively looking for another job, and although I told her I'd search for one myself, she said it was more important for me to be at Lauder, playing hockey. If I got drafted, it would make it all worth it.

I nodded at Imogen. I'd planned to tell her tonight when we sneaked into the theater room, but Ford had spilled the news at dinner.

Mr. Jacobs leaned back in his chair. He was an intimidating man. Not only his size, but the way he presented himself to others. He definitely had plans for Ford that didn't include hockey, and when a future in hockey did come up, he always said it wasn't a career. Ford told me he and his dad had come to some agreement that he could play in college, then hang up his skates. I'd seen the disappointment on Ford's face when he told me, especially since I said I was entering the draft.

"Why?" Mr. Jacobs asked. "I just talked to the chancellor, and he told me what an outstanding student you are. Why wouldn't you attend college?"

Since everyone but Imogen believed that my family was Langley Wines, I didn't know how to answer. I definitely couldn't tell him the truth—that I had to enter the draft so I could start making money for my family. "I love playing hockey. School will always be there."

It was a lie I told myself often. In another life, maybe I could've gone to college, gotten the education Mr. Jacobs had so I could try to give Imogen his level of wealth. I knew I was smart and already had schools reaching out to me about playing for them. But a scholarship to a college wouldn't allow me to provide for my family for another four years at least.

I looked at Imogen across from me, but she concentrated on her dinner, pushing her broccoli around the plate. I wanted to assure her that this was the best move for us. I'd play a game I loved, and while she was making something of herself at college, I'd be building our future. I wouldn't be able to give her all of what she'd grown up with, but a helluva lot more than I could right then. But that conversation would have to wait until that night.

"I think you're being foolish," Mr. Jacobs said.

"Everyone has a different path in life." Mrs. Jacobs smiled at me. She lowered her fork and ran her hand down my arm. "How exciting for you. Do you have a specific team you want to play for?"

"I'd love to stay in New York," I answered, peeking at Imogen through my eyelashes.

"I think it's great. Way to do what you want." Ford avoided eye contact with his dad. "Don't listen to what everyone else thinks."

"What is that supposed to mean?" Mr. Jacobs was quick to question his son.

The closer we got to graduation, the more I noticed Mr. Jacobs and Ford at odds. Mr. Jacobs was never at games, and Ford was always mumbling under his breath when his dad was around. Imogen had told me they were fighting constantly about Ford's future.

While the two of them argued over my decision, Mrs. Jacobs told Imogen, Morgan, and me to get dessert and go to the theater or game room and she'd send Ford on when he was done talking to his dad. Which was music to my ears.

Bernie scooped some truffle thing he'd made with custard, cake, and fruit into three bowls, and we left. I hated leaving Ford with his dad to have yet another argument, but Mrs. Jacobs had made her wishes known.

"I'm going to my room," Morgan said when we hit the stairs.

We waited for her to shut her door before heading to the theater room. Imogen put on a movie just in case someone came in, and we sat in the back row as usual.

"When were you going to tell me?" she asked.

"Tonight. I wanted you to know first. I'm sorry. Ford saw me meeting with my agent and… you know Ford. He won't stop prodding when he wants to know something."

She nodded.

I put my dessert on the chair next to me. "I'm doing this for us too. I mean, I have no choice, my family needs the money, but while you're at school getting your degree, I'll get a head start on building our life together."

A smile crept up her lips. "What?"

"Why do you think I want to stay in New York?"

"Because of your mom, Trinity, and Julien."

I turned toward her, running my palm along her cheek and down to her neck. "Because of you mostly. I want to be where you are."

She blushed. I knew she doubted me a lot and I couldn't blame her. I had to be the bigger man and tell Ford. Stop playing this game we'd been playing for months.

"I'm going to tell him."

Her eyes peeked up at me. We both knew it was time. Things were getting serious with us. "You don't have—"

I put my finger to her lips. "Yeah, I do."

I bent over to kiss her, but the door flew open and Ford stood there. I could tell the conversation with his dad hadn't gone well, and now he'd just found me with his sister.

"What the hell is this?" he roared.

There was no point in lying—he'd seen my hands on his sister—so I stood. "I have something I need to tell you."

"You said I could trust you. Are you fucking her?"

"Ford!" Imogen yelled and stood at my side.

I wrapped my arm around her and pulled her to my side, my heart thumping like a driving bass. "I love her."

"What?" Ford's eyes scrunched, and he shook his head, but I saw the fight leave him. He looked defeated. Maybe I'd caught *him at the right time. Maybe his dad had drained all the anger from him. He turned his attention to Imogen. "And you?"*

She nodded and looked up at me with her cheek on my chest. "Me too. I love him."

I wanted to kiss her so badly right then, but I wasn't an idiot.

Ford ran a hand through his hair. "Fuck, man."

"I'm really sorry. I should have told you sooner, but... it just happened."

He huffed and sighed, staring at his shoes for a moment before raising his head. "You fuck with her, and I'll be the first one to beat your ass."

"It's not like that."

"I'm trusting you not to hurt her." He held my gaze.

I nodded.

"And if you think that you're going to ditch me every weekend for my sister, you're crazy. And I am not being your wingman and getting stuck with Cici."

Imogen and I laughed. I couldn't believe he was taking it as well as he was. At that moment, I wanted to tell him all of it. Confess that I wasn't related in any way to Langley Wines. But I figured one thing at a time.

"Promise," I say. "You're really okay with this?"

He sighed. "I'd rather you than anyone else."

That sentence alone made me realize that Ford and I were those kinds of friends. The ones you trust with anything, the ones you have for life.

"Warner!" Imogen waves her hand in front of my face.

I glance at her. "Shit. Sorry."

"You missed the turn."

I do a quick U-turn at the next light and pull into the gym parking lot. Taking the keys out of the ignition, I sit there for a moment.

"What were you thinking about?" Her hand is on the door handle.

"You don't want to know." I climb out of my SUV and grab my bag from the back.

"You can't drive and zone out like that."

She's at my side when we enter the gym. Tabitha, the girl at the front desk who also teaches the yoga classes, smiles at me until she sees the film crew behind me. She clams up even though Imogen mentioned at some point this week that she'd gotten the okay from the gym to film here.

"Hi, Warner," she says, interrupting my conversation with Imogen. Which is good. I don't want to dredge up our past right now.

"Tabitha, this is Imogen and the film crew. They're just going to film me and no one else." I scan my membership card and we all walk in.

Her eyes remain fixed on the cameras, though she doesn't respond.

I'm surprised to find a couple of guys in the weights area. Usually at this time of the day, it's just me and Lyle, a seventy-two-year-old Vietnam veteran who likes to recap all my games with me. I've developed a kinship with him and managed to bust through his tough exterior. But he's not here today.

The camera guys are getting set up and Imogen is clearly annoyed, huffing when she sits on a bench out of the shot. Two guys approach her almost immediately as she sits there, legs crossed and typing on her phone. I watch from the sidelines for a minute until I realize they're all pulling out their cell phones as though they're going to exchange numbers.

"She's off-limits," I say, wedging myself between them.

"What? You already have a chance with any girl you want. Didn't your mom ever teach you to share?"

Imogen's eyes narrow on me. "I am not his and I am not off-limits," she says to them with a flirtatious vibe that makes the vein in my neck throb.

Yeah, we're not playing this game.

"Excuse us," I say to her. I walk a few paces away and call the guys over. "Listen, consider her like a cherished childhood toy. No one shares that toy. You got it?" I raise an eyebrow.

They both chuckle.

"What's in it for us?" one asks.

I've seen these two around the gym a couple of times. I think they're best friends called the two Matts. "You can get in the video if you want. Spot me."

Both their eyes light up and I don't need to say anything more.

So I work out with the two Matts, who are definitely stronger than me, but we both get what we want in the end —they get on camera, and they don't get Imogen.

Once I'm finished, I shower and change into casual clothes.

"Breakfast?" I ask Imogen when I emerge from the changing room.

"Nope. We're not even close to having a meal together at a restaurant."

"You have to eat."

She sighs, and her stomach rumbles at the exact right moment. She looks down and places her hand there. "Traitor. Fine, we can get bagels, but we go Dutch, and we do not sit at a table."

I laugh, climbing into my SUV. "So you eat carbs?"

She narrows her eyes at me. "You can stop with the jokes."

It might only be bagels, but any time I get to spend with Imogen can't be taken for granted. I smile like the lunatic I am all the way to the bagel shop.

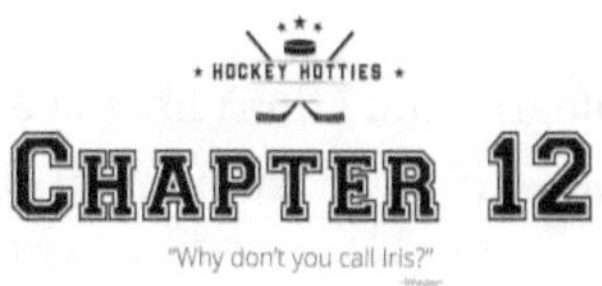

CHAPTER 12

Imogen

arner uses his charm to sway the cashier into allowing him to pay for our bagels and coffees. We leave the camera crew at a table and stroll down the boardwalk along the beach.

"Thank you." I lift my coffee before taking a sip.

"I would've paid for a fancy breakfast place if you'd let me." He takes a big bite of his bagel that's overflowing with cream cheese.

"So, no special diet?" I nod at the bagel in his hand, then point toward the cream cheese on the corner of his mouth.

He wipes it and smiles at me. "Not during the season. I burn off enough calories from practices and games."

We continue to walk in silence for a bit. At least the scenery is different from the last time I went on a walk with him. Back then, we were swallowed up by soaring skyscrapers and tons of concrete.

"Gen..."

I distract myself by sipping my iced latte. It's clear from the use of my shortened name that he wants to broach the past again, and I can't go there right now. "Can we pretend you're just a hockey player and I'm just the hype girl having to follow you?"

"You can't keep ignoring the fact that I want to apologize properly."

"You can apologize, but I don't have to accept it."

"True, but you won't even let me get it out."

I stop and turn to face him. "Go ahead. If this ends you having to talk about it."

His shoulders slump. "I'm sorry. There's no excuse for what I did. It's my most regretted decision, and I wish I could transport us back in time and change it."

I nod. "Thank you for the apology." I try to keep my voice even.

"But you don't accept it."

I walk again, hating standing still, hating facing him when I don't hate him as much as I should. "I do accept it. It just doesn't change anything. I'm not going to guilt you for the rest of our lives. I appreciate the apology and we can move on."

"Move on as what?"

"Warner..." I wait a moment to collect my thoughts. "You're under some assumption that there could be a future between us. That's not going to happen. There's too much baggage. Too much has happened between us. Our trust was broken, and it can't be fixed."

"Why? I still see it, Gen... the way you look at me. It's the same way you used to across the dinner table."

I move my gaze away from him. He wants real? I'll give it to him. "I wish I could carve out the spot you dug for yourself in my heart. You have no idea how many times I tried. Sometimes I forget to remember what you did. Sometimes I make up excuses that you were just a teenager—too young and scared to do the right thing. But I've never felt as alone as I did then. I can't put myself in that situation again."

Hurt fills his dark eyes. He opens his mouth to speak,

but a swarm of kids call his name and rush us from farther down the boardwalk.

A little redheaded boy with glasses turns around to show us the back of the jersey he's wearing. "Number thirty-four!"

Warner seems to push aside his hurt and turns on his charm when the mother rushes over, apologizing the entire time until she reaches us.

"It's okay." He places his bagel and coffee on a nearby bench and pats his pockets. "I don't have a pen or anything."

The mom drops her oversized purse on the bench, rummaging through it. I look at my small purse hanging from my arm and wonder when that transformation happens. Do you go up a size after each kid or do you ditch the small purse for a huge one as soon as you have your firstborn?

"Here you go." She holds up a Sharpie as though it's a prize. I'm not surprised she has one.

"Great. Want me to sign your jersey for you?" Warner squats down and opens the Sharpie before signing his name on the jersey. Then he looks up at me. "Do you have paper?"

Why is he asking me and not the woman who's ready for war with the monster purse?

"No."

He digs into his pocket, finding the receipt from our bagels. He signs it and hands it to the boy. "Just in case."

Then the other boys are rushing forward with pieces of paper the mom with the giant purse is handing out. Warner smiles and asks them if they play. He interacts with ease, but I guess his younger brother has probably helped him learn how to interact with kids.

"Is she your girlfriend?" the redhead whispers.

Warner looks back at me and smirks. "No."

"But she's so pretty."

I want to squat down and hug him for making my day a little brighter.

"I know, right? But she's way out of my league."

The entire group of boys is surrounding Warner, and the mom smiles over their little heads at me.

"Nah, you're Warner Langley," one of them says.

Warner shrugs. "That doesn't mean anything. She doesn't care how I perform on the ice."

"She should date you just for the number of goals you made two nights ago," another kid chimes in, giving me a nasty look.

"Ah, remember you can play awesome on the ice, but you gotta be a good person. Treat others with respect, how you want to be treated." He pokes the redhead in the chest but moves his finger around, so everyone knows the advice is for all of them. "Be a good teammate."

"Does that mean you're not those things if she doesn't want to date you?" the redhead asks.

The mom laughs. "That's enough questions. Thank Mr. Langley for his time."

The group of boys step back, all saying thank you at once.

"Thank you very much. You're very kind to do all this." She smiles at him.

"Of course. In fact, give me your number and I'll see what I can do about tickets for the next game."

"Shut up!" the redhead exclaims, eyes wide, mouth hanging open.

"No way!"

"Awesome!"

The boys' excitement is contagious. I'll make sure they

get tickets myself. Warner accepts the mom's number and I pluck it out of his hand.

"I'll be in touch," I tell her.

We say our goodbyes to the boys and turn back around to find that the camera crew must have been filming our interaction.

"No good deed ever goes unnoticed," Warner mumbles.

Guilt tugs at my insides for dimming the light in his eyes with my truth, but I had to be honest. I can't afford to get wrapped up in this man again. It almost destroyed me once. I don't know that I'd survive it a second time.

THE NEXT STOP of the day is an advertising campaign for the watch company he models for.

The minute we walk in, everyone treats Warner like the superstar he is. Fawning over his latest game stats, telling him how they have donuts from his favorite place at the craft table. He does that fist-knocking thing to every guy on set and hugs every woman. By the time we make it to the makeup room, I'm annoyed, but can't put my finger on why exactly.

The makeup artist comes in, eyeing me up and down before staring at Warner through the mirror. "Who's this?"

"Imogen Jacobs, meet Mario Cruz." Warner motions between us.

"I wasn't asking for a name, more of a clarification." He steps over and offers me his hand.

I shake it. "I work for the Fury. Just one of the people following Warner around for the day."

"Oh... how nice." He raises his perfectly shaped eyebrows at Warner through the mirror and opens his makeup case. "Sometimes I'm afraid I'll turn you ugly instead of the other way around."

I huff and Mario glances at me before focusing his attention on Warner.

"You need something to drink?" Warner asks.

"No. I'm fine." I take a seat on the couch and lean back and cross my legs.

"Guess who isn't here yet?" Mario says to Warner as though he's about to dish out a big piece of gossip.

"Seriously? She messes with the schedule every damn time." There's annoyance in Warner's voice that I don't hear very often. "I don't have time to wait around for her to grace us with her presence."

Mario must notice my confused expression because he's quick to explain. "They do all the ads together. You know, beautiful woman, gorgeous male."

"I assume we're talking about Aria Chand?" I say.

The million ads I've seen of her and Warner come to mind. Them on a yacht, them shopping in Los Angeles, in front of the Christmas tree at Rockefeller. I guess Warner can act as well as he plays hockey because every billboard or print ad I've seen looks as if they're in love.

"She couldn't be on time if she was hosting *Saturday Night Live*," Warner grumbles.

Mario touches Warner's shoulder, giggling. "Did you hear when she did? She was late, and those people had the balls to send her home. Maybe if they did that once here, she'd figure out how to be on time."

"They won't." He frowns, and his gaze reaches mine in the mirror.

People have been shipping them together for years. I get it, the dark brooding bad boy and the beautiful, sophisticated woman. I was jealous the first time I saw them together. It felt like I was swallowing jagged glass.

"We're not a couple." Warner stands and pulls off the white piece of paper around his neck.

"Hey, I wasn't finished." Mario holds a small eyebrow brush.

"I'm fine." Warner walks out.

I stand from the couch.

"Boy, you sure get his undies all wadded up, don't you?" Mario comes over and elbows me in the side. "Tell me the tea. Who are you really?"

"I'm the hype woman for the Florida Fury. That's all."

I follow Warner down the hallway. The camera crew is already in front of him to track his every step.

"She's not here yet?" Warner says to a woman sitting in the chair I envision directors in.

She finishes chewing the donut she's eating and swallows. "She's a few minutes out, I'm told. Got caught in traffic. Not used to being here. Blah, blah, blah. Let's remember you dictated for us to come to you. She's making the special trip."

Warner practically growls. "I have plans. Can we speed this up? Get the lighting figured out in the meantime... something?"

The woman looks at him as though she's placating him. "We need the both of you."

He tugs on my sleeve, pulling me to his side. "You can use her."

I pull my sleeve out of his hold. "Excuse me?"

The woman looks me over. "Just sit and wait. Eat the donuts you love so much."

Warner's hands fist at his side. "Janice, I have something to do after this that's pressing."

I hate that I wonder what he has to do and who it might be with. It's none of my business.

"I'll make it snappy when she gets here. Promise." But Janice must see something in his face because she sighs. "Fine. The two of you up in front." She points, but I stay in place.

"Imogen, come on. You're just Aria's stand-in." Warner holds his hand out to me.

I shake my head, but he doesn't retract his hand.

"Please. I'll make this up to you."

I exhale a deep breath. Him and those damn eyes. "Fine, but you can make it up to me by not doing anything for me."

"How do you want us?" Warner asks Janice, ignoring my jab.

"You're sitting in that chair and your wrist is cocked to look at your watch. She's standing above you, leaning over your shoulder and whispering something in your ear."

That's easy enough. The two of us get into position. God, the closer I get to him, the more I can smell his cologne. He smells good. My eyes close of their own accord and a flash of our naked bodies running along one another's flashes in my mind.

Janice comes over and moves my leg up on the arm of the chair and brings his arm around my thigh so he's touching my shin with the arm without the watch on it. "You have to lean in close like you're telling him something very dirty that'll get him to ditch whatever appointment he has, hence him checking his watch."

Warner's hand runs up my thigh and back down. "Relax. This is just for lighting. Nothing more," he whispers.

I suppress the shiver that threatens to rack my body and lean in close.

"Feel free to talk dirty to me," he says. "On second thought, I don't want my dick to get hard."

I sputter out a laugh. Leaning in close, I can't help myself. "Telling you I'm not wearing any panties right now wouldn't make you hard, would it? Or the fact I'm completely bare under my blouse and pants?" My nipples pebble.

The photographer takes a few test shots.

"Great, you two. Let me check some things." Janice walks away with the photographer, and they go to look at the monitor set up at the side.

"Damn, Gen," he says, shifting in the seat.

"I'm here! Everyone, I'm here!" a female voice with a slight accent announces. As Aria comes out of the darkness and sees me with Warner, she stops in her tracks. "Who are you?"

"Aria, you're late again," he says.

"Who's this?" She points and looks at who I assume is her assistant, from the number of bags she's carrying and the flustered look on her face.

"I have plans. Can you please get ready?" Warner asks.

"Tell her to get out of my spot," she snipes while she walks away.

I gladly step away and back toward the camera crew.

Warner's cell phone rings. He silences it and walks over to me. "Do you mind holding this? I forgot I had it on me."

I take it. "Sure."

Forty-five minutes later, Aria walks on set, giving me a nasty look. She kisses Warner on the cheek and says something about how muscular he's getting. I inwardly roll my eyes.

Janice puts them in a similar position to the one we were in, but I'm sure Aria pulls it off much better than I did. They end up going through four different setups, Janice saying they want a sequence of events. The whole thing ends with Warner's watch on the nightstand of a bed and Aria in a man's dress shirt walking into a room. At least I didn't have to actually see him in a bed with her.

When the shoot is finally over, Warner shrugs on his shirt and talks to Janice and a few others. His phone buzzes in my hand, and I glance down and see the name Iris on his screen. I'm guessing she's his important plans for tonight. I let it go to voice mail and I'm forced to admit to myself that I'm seething with jealousy.

"Hey, you ready?" He's in a much more chipper mood than before.

I hand him his phone. "Sure." I push his phone into his chest with more force than necessary.

He glances down at the screen, but says nothing, pocketing his phone.

We walk out of the studio, say our goodbyes to the camera crew, and I slide into his SUV.

"I was thinking we could do dinner?" He turns the key in the ignition.

"Only if it involves a protein bar from the gas station."

He chuckles. "What?"

"I already told you, we're not going on a date."

He glances over when we reach a stop sign, then presses hard on the gas, making my back plaster to the seat. He's silent the entire ride home, and I can't get out of his SUV fast enough when he pulls into his driveway beside my car.

"I don't know why you're so mad. You said you had important plans tonight." I climb out of his SUV and walk to my car.

"With you. My plans were to take you to dinner." There's

an edge to his tone, like he has the nerve to be pissed off at me.

I open my car door. "Why don't you call Iris?"

Then I climb into my car and drive off, effectively getting the last word in.

It doesn't feel as great as I thought it would.

CHAPTER 13

Warner

*D*rake comes up to me after the game, mindful that Ford is ahead of us because he speaks in a low voice. I know where his loyalty lies, but I've given the guy more assists than Ford in the last few games, plus, we seem to be able to always know where the other one is on the ice.

"I've never played with someone who can backhand with the control you have," he says while we walk down the hallway toward the locker room.

"I've never played with someone who has your stamina."

Drake laughs. "Conditioning. I've been doing a helluva lot more of it since they signed Jet. Gotta keep my starting line position."

I understand what he's saying. I sense Drake and I are the same type of person. We don't do second place, but both of our times to hang up the skates will come. It's inevitable.

"Listen." He stops me outside the locker room. "Saige and I are having a dinner party next month that rare weekend that we don't have a game. Do you want to come?"

"Dinner party, huh?"

He shrugs. "Ford will be there, but I'll talk to him."

"Nah." I shake my head. "Thanks for the invitation, but I'm gonna pass."

He peeks into the locker room and puts his hand on my chest to keep me from going in. "I don't know why you two hate one another. Ford is pretty tight lipped about it, but it's making our line suffer. He's pissed every time I shoot you the puck, and you two avoid one another on the ice like you're each other's competition. We can't win the Cup if you guys continue on this way. The dinner party is a way for me to get you two to mend fences."

"The problems of a captain," I say. Drake's supposed to be the man who keeps our locker room drama-free.

"You'd think they would've consulted me before trading for you." He chuckles and pounds his fist into my chest lightly. "Just think about it. I'll deal with Ford."

He disappears into the locker room, and I follow a minute later, noticing Ford and Drake in conversation. Ford whips his head in my direction, and it's clear he's seething.

I understand that Drake's in a tough position, but he's right. We aren't going to win the Cup if Ford and I don't get on the same page. If we can't figure out how to play together on the same line, we're screwed.

At my locker by Cory and Kane, I sit down to take off my skates.

"I hate meet and greets," Kane says. "It's like an excuse to let women grope you."

"Is that a bad thing?" Cory asks with a chuckle. I don't know if he's ever done a meet and greet, and maybe he won't care that he has to hug every single woman who comes through. Given the way he's screwing his way through the puck bunnies these days, my bet is he won't mind.

While Kane gives Jet the lowdown on how they work, I glance at Ford and Drake, seeing Maksim Petrov is now talking to each of them. Those three are like the three musketeers of the Florida Fury, and now I'm causing trouble in their friendship, which was never my intention. I never wanted to lose my friendship with Ford, but when push came to shove, he had to choose a side. I can't blame him for taking his sister's. Maybe that's why he never wanted us to get together in the first place. He didn't want to be in the situation I put him in. But he seems to forget that he put me in a situation I didn't want to be in either.

Our coach at Lauder had a friend who coached at a public high school and organized a scrimmage between the two teams. Both of us were the best of the best for our respective leagues.

Ford and I were talking about a delicate situation as we headed to the rink. "Come on, man, Mrs. Iverson loves you. You're the only one who can get a copy of the test, and if we don't get the McGregor brothers to pass Greek mythology, they can't play, and we won't win the big trophy our senior year." He pounded me on the shoulders.

"If they want the test, they can get it themselves."

Could I get a copy of the test? Probably. And pretty easily, because Ford was right, Mrs. Iverson had a soft spot for me. She'd asked me to stay on my first day and told me that if I ever needed anything, to go to her. Stealing the test would feel like deceiving a good friend. But I also knew Lauder had brought me on to win a championship and that wasn't going to happen without the McGregor brothers.

"They'd fuck it up and get suspended," Ford said.

"Why don't we just tutor them?" It was my last grasp for any other reason not to steal the test. I was smart enough and patient enough to tutor. Hell, I had been Trinity's tutor since she was in pre-K and came home crying that she didn't know her ABCs.

Just then, the McGregor brothers bulldozed by us onto the ice, arguing about almond milk and whether it was true that if you put almonds in a grinder, it would produce milk.

"Can't we just cut it open like a coconut?" one said to the other.

"No, I tried to cut one open the other day and no milk in there."

I looked at Ford and nodded. Yeah, tutoring wasn't an option. The McGregors were our biggest defenders, and if their grades slipped any further, they couldn't play.

"I'll see what I can do." I figured at least that would buy me some time.

Ford hit me in the chest. "Don't forget the answer key," he said, then skated over to our side.

The other team was already on the other side of the ice, taking practice shots. I got in line but did a double take at one of the players. Crap. A kid I'd played with when I was little had recognized me and was skating over. My pulse quickened, and I skated a little away from our group to give us some privacy.

"Shit, Langley." I felt eyes on me from what felt like every direction, but we were far enough away that no one would hear us over the skating and slapping of pucks against sticks. "Did your mom marry some rich fuck or some shit?"

Payton Walker hadn't grown as tall as I would have thought. When we were younger, he was the bigger, taller, and faster kid. When his family decided to move to Minnesota, where hockey was taken more seriously, everyone thought that one day we'd see Payton in the pros. But I had at least three inches and probably thirty pounds on him.

"I thought you moved?" I asked, hoping to steer the conversation in his direction.

"We did, but my dad's old company needed him and made an offer he couldn't refuse, so we came back." He hit me in the chest. "I'm only a few blocks from you now. What the hell are you doing going to Lauder?"

I shrugged, unsure how to answer him.

"You're the one I heard about?"

"What?" I looked over at my teammates.

Ford kept glancing over between shots.

"You're the one who got a scholarship to play? My teammates couldn't stop talking about some kid from the neighborhood who was playing up here." He looked at a friend skating by. "Hey, Zele, get over here."

The guy stopped and skated over. "What?"

"This is the guy I was telling you about. He and I used to play together when we were young."

"You're the scholarship kid?" He didn't say it too loud, but still, I scoured my teammates to make sure no one had heard.

I nodded.

He leaned in close. "How's the pussy at Lauder? I bet it's all smooth shaved and smells like fucking cake."

As if timing couldn't have been worse, Imogen and Cici barreled down the stairs into the arena, Imogen eyeing me as she found a seat in the first row. I couldn't strip my gaze from her. Ever since we'd come out as a couple, things had been better than ever. I walked a fine line between spending time with her and Ford, happy that she didn't have the same lunch period as me because reserving that time exclusively for Ford had helped keep our friendship strong.

"Oh shit, cake with whipped cream and twenty-four karat sprinkles, I bet." Zele was talking more to Payton than to me. "Lucky fuck."

I turned back from eyeing Imogen to see Zele had gone back to his team while Payton was still at my side.

"Let's go out sometime. Introduce me to her friend?" He nodded in the girls' direction.

"Sure, I'll catch you after the game and give you my number."

Thankfully, Coach called me over and we said good luck to each other before skating to our designated sides.

"What the fuck? Talking to the enemy?" Ford asked, his eyes on Payton.

I often wondered why Ford always felt so threatened by everyone else. I wasn't sure if he'd ever had a true-blue friend besides me.

"Just a kid I used to play with when I was younger."

"Where'd you play with him?" Peter asked, his tone clearly indicating that he thought the guys on the other side of the ice were beneath us somehow.

"The lake... you wouldn't know it. Up north. He just moved down here."

"You played with a kid who attends public high school?" Peter continued.

"Give the kid a break, his dad lost his job." My lie wasn't completely a lie, but close enough. I just needed to get us on to another topic.

"So fucking judgmental, Peter." One of the McGregor brothers hit him in the shoulder as Coach came over with his clipboard.

"Okay, enough socializing." Coach looked us all over. "Who invited the fans?"

Ford raised his hand. "I got outvoted."

"We all know Langley plays better when she's here," someone chirped, and everyone agreed.

Even Ford shook his head, but I hadn't thought about it until that moment. They were right. I'd had more goals, more assists since Imogen and I came out as a couple.

"It's true, Coach," Ford said.

"Your sister is fine, Ford, but her friend is a little crazy. If she starts pounding the glass again, she'll be removed."

"Noted."

Then Coach went in the middle, talking to the starting line about the play he wanted. Of course, it was some combination of Ford and me because we were just too fucking good together.

After Coach was finished, I skated over to Imogen and Cici, stopping at the glass. I pointed at Cici. "Behave yourself or you're out."

She laughed and leaned back in the seat.

Imogen walked to the glass, her hands outstretched until she placed her palms there. I put my hand over hers.

"Thanks for coming," I said loudly enough for her to hear.

"I'm your biggest fan." She unzipped her coat, and it took everything in me not to get hard in that moment. She wore a deep V-neck T-shirt that had "#34 Scores Here" written on it.

"Ford's gonna have a shit fit," I said, soaking in the view of her tits snug in the tight fabric. "Keep the coat on until later."

She giggled. "Go score me some goals."

I winked. "Every one of them is for you."

She licked her lips like she did every time I scored. Like it was a promise of what was to come after the game. I couldn't deny it, I was falling for Imogen. Hell, I'd already fallen, who was I kidding?

"Fuck, look at all these women." Cory's voice sounds as though there's a little bit of awe in it as we enter the room where the meet and greet will be held.

His voice warps me back to reality and out of the past.

Sadness coats the inside of my heart as I see Imogen. She's not mine. There's no licking lips or promises of kisses after games anymore. Instead, it's all business, so I head over to my spot at the long table, Cory and Kane to my left.

Business is business, but if the flashbacks keep haunting me, I'll never move on. Imogen might have given me her forgiveness the other day, but not enough for another chance. Which means I have to fight a little harder. Everything I got in life is because I didn't quit. I don't plan on starting now.

CHAPTER 14

Imogen

"It's kind of disgusting, no?" I ask Jana, who's leaning against the back wall. "Half these women have wedding rings on."

Jana laughs and looks at me. "Someone sounds jealous."

"No." I sip the Diet Coke I still have from the game.

"You are so."

Truth is, the whole Iris thing threw me. As mad as I am at Warner, I know he's not the type to play a woman. Especially since he saw men doing it to his mother over and over again growing up. He wouldn't be hell-bent on going after me if he had another girl, but that doesn't mean there's not a woman who's after him. I wonder if she's a puck bunny he calls when he's in a specific town.

Besides, I shouldn't even care. I've made it clear to him that nothing is going to happen between us. My brain knows Warner isn't any good for me. My heart hasn't gotten the memo.

"I just don't understand why a woman would ask them to sign above her breast when there's a kid right behind her in line."

Jana smiles. "It's okay, you can be jealous. I would be if I had any interest in one of those three." She nods toward the table where Warner, Cory, and Kane sit.

If Jana wasn't my boss, I might call her out on her shit. She thinks no one saw her and Kane on the dance floor at Ford's wedding. Or noticed the fact they disappeared together. But she is my boss and I really want to keep my job, so I don't mention it.

"The other day when I was with him, he had me hold his phone and a woman called."

Jana shrugs. "Probably his mother."

"No." I shake my head.

She turns toward me, ignoring the fans. "How do you know?"

"Who puts their mom's first name in the phone?"

"Maybe it's an aunt or a stepmom or something."

I shake my head.

"Well, Miss Know-It-All, you could enlighten me on how you know, or we can play this game all night." The coy look on her face gives away what she's trying to accomplish.

"Okay, fine, we were involved once upon a time."

She snaps her finger and points at me. "I knew it." She raises her hand. "I just want to go on the record and say that I could probably be a medium."

"A medium talks to dead people," I deadpan.

"Yes, a dead person told me."

I shake my head and she laughs. For a moment, Kane stops signing and glances over.

"Let's go somewhere quieter," she says, sliding her arm through mine. "We have to discuss something."

She leads me out of the room, but not before Warner and I lock eyes.

Jana takes me up to her office. I take a seat while she brings the projector screen down from the ceiling and shows footage from the day I spent with Warner.

"We're doing this now?"

"I'm not going to sit down there all night." She clicks the remote. "I love when the boys come up to you guys when you're walking down the beach. I assume you got them tickets?"

"Yeah, had to book them on a nonschool night. They're coming this weekend."

"Perfect." She taps her pointer finger on her bottom lip. "Let's make sure the kids get into the locker room after the guys have showered and dressed. They can chat with Warner, get some pictures and photos with some of the players. Maybe you can give them a behind-the-scenes tour."

My forehead wrinkles. "Do what?"

She gives me what seems to be her favorite coy expression. "You'll see it when he does it."

"And if he doesn't?"

"Then he's not the guy I think he might be." She presses Play on the remote again. Once the scene from the beach is done, it flips to the photo shoot. "I love this one. It's really a shame I have to cut it out. Do you want me to save it for you?"

I watch as I position myself behind him on the set and lean in to whisper in his ear.

"What did you tell him?" She pauses and my cheeks flush as I remember Warner's reaction. "Never mind." She giggles. "You can keep that between you two." She keeps it paused, resting the remote under her chin, staring at the giant screen. "I'm sure you don't want to hear this, but you two make a gorgeous couple. You just fit."

I look from her to the screen and my heart squeezes. "Did. Past tense."

She shakes her head at me. "One day, I'm going to get the whole story out of you."

"Probably." I sigh. She's relentless.

She turns her whole body in her seat to face me. "Want to tell me anything right now?"

"Let's just finish this." I grab the remote from her and press Play.

It continues and Aria comes in. Talk about a couple who fit. They'd be like the king and queen of modeling if those two got together. I don't pause or stop the video and it ends after he gets in his SUV, pulling away from the studio. I turn it off and drop the remote between us.

"Looks like a fun day. We can definitely chop it into a five- or ten-minute video. Maybe do a few versions... one can play before a game, another we could put on our socials."

I type some notes into my phone. "Great. I'll work on it first thing in the morning."

"What do you have planned next?"

"The meet and greet that's going on now. Then I thought about doing some contests on social media, and the winners get to have a three-minute-and-forty-second interview with Warner. Sort of an 'ask me anything.' Maybe on one of the weekends he's home. We could set it up outside the arena and spectators would come to watch... and, of course, share it all over socials for bragging rights."

"Love that."

A knock on the door startles us, but we both smile, seeing Cory Freeman in the side window. He gives us a short wave and Jana waves him in.

"You guys just left us down there to fend for ourselves. They're like vultures. Not that I mind." He chuckles and sits down across from Jana.

Jana leans back in her chair. "Yes, I hear you're some-what of a ladies' man these days."

Before he can respond, Warner walks in and stares at the giant screen.

"We were just watching you, figuring out a way to market that gorgeous face." Jana grins.

Warner shakes his head, appearing uncomfortable.

"I feel slightly offended no one wants this gorgeous face." Cory smiles brightly, showing off his perfectly white teeth that I'm positive is part of what the women must love.

Jana pinches his cheeks. "One day we will, but we gotta get the freshness off of you. Maybe next year. As long as you're still single."

He balks. Warner sits in the chair next to me and I stiffen a bit at his proximity. A second later, Kane enters, and Jana freezes for a moment as he rests his back along the wall.

"Why do I have to be single?" Cory asks.

Jana shrugs. "Single sells."

"I don't think that's true. Women fawn over Ford and his baby girl every time she comes to the games."

Cory has a point, but as I open my mouth, Jana answers. "Because they're convincing themselves Lena is his nanny and not his wife." She gestures toward Warner. "Take Langley for a second. If he and Imogen got their shit together—"

"Jana." I lower my voice to a threat, but she doesn't care.

Cory just winks at me. He's definitely got game.

"People wouldn't give a shit about him. I mean, they would—there are always those women who think they have the power to break up a couple—but the majority of women want to know he's available."

"I had no idea." Cory rubs his jaw with his palm.

"Believe me, as a woman, it's shameful to admit. But it's the truth. Putting a wedding ring on will do one of two things. Turn on the demented women who don't care that you're taken because you've proven you can commit—even though those cheating with them would actually mean the opposite." She rolls her eyes. "Or make women not as interested in you because they respect the fact you chose someone else." She places her hand on Cory's shoulder.

"Man, I'm just gonna sit up here for sex education class. Tell me, why hasn't the girl I met at Ford's wedding called me?" I can tell he's disappointed.

"Jesus Christ, we came up here to see if you two wanted to head to Carmelo's?" Kane interrupts. "Freeman, man up and call the woman and ask her yourself."

"You make it sound so easy. I've never done this shit before."

"Clearly." Kane pushes off the wall. "Who's going and who's not?"

Jana sets her gaze on Kane. "Jeez, calm down. There's nothing wrong with Cory asking for advice from two qualified sources."

She's definitely my idol. I know something went down with them the night of the wedding, but she can stare at Kane with disdain for hours and not give herself away. While I purposely don't allow myself to look at Warner—even though I feel his eyes blazing into the side of my head—because I know I'll give myself away.

"Qualified?" Kane says condescendingly and chuckles.

Warner's quick to stand. "Let's go. We'll be over at Carmelo's if you want to join us. Come on, Jet."

Cory stands. "It's been a pleasure." After the other two leave the room, he turns around and rubs his hands together. "Don't listen to them. They each have their own deep-rooted issues with the two of you."

"FREEMAN!" Kane bellows from down the hall.

"I should get going. Carmelo's. Come on, ladies." He winks one final time, turns on his heel, and walks out the door. "Shit, guys, wait up." We hear Cory jog down the hall.

Jana looks at me. "I'm not going."

I shake my head like I wasn't even fathoming the idea. Although it's becoming harder and harder for me to keep my distance from Warner. Jana has something for Kane, I just know it, but she has willpower like a model when it comes to food. Kane's the big ice cream sundae that she politely passes and tells everyone dairy makes her stomach upset. While I'm lactose intolerant and I'll choose to suffer through the consequences.

"How do you do it?" I ask.

She cocks her head. "Do what?"

"Act like Kane doesn't faze you?"

She laughs and presses the button to put the screen back in place and turns on the lights. "He doesn't."

Man, she's good. I think I could hook her up to a lie detector test and she'd pass.

"I'll walk you out to your car," I say, moving off the topic.

"I have more work to do. Don't worry, I'll call Fred when I want to go home. He'll walk me out, but thank you."

As I pack up, I wonder if I should call the security officer, Fred, to walk me out, but no. I'll be fine.

"I'm really happy about the work you've done, Imogen. I told my dad to trust me, and so far, you've made me look extremely good. Thank you."

"Thanks, Jana. That means so much."

She smiles and shoos me with her hands. "Now go and head to Carmelo's. You deserve a drink."

"I think a glass of wine back at my place is all I need. See you tomorrow."

"Yep. Night."

I head down the hall toward the elevator. I have no idea how Jana works here by herself all the time. Every office is dark, and the only lights are the dim ones that come on as I walk. I round the bend to the elevator bank and press the down button. As I wait, every noise has the small hairs on the back of my neck on edge. I swear Jana is fearless. To be her for a day.

I slide my hand into my purse and grab my pepper spray just in case.

Thankfully, the elevator doors open. The car is vacant, so I scurry in and press the button to get me to the parking lot. Maybe there are still some players going home and I can find one of them to walk out with. I should've called Fred.

It doesn't take long for the elevator to reach ground level, and I glance to the right and left before stepping off and heading out of the building to my car. I walk as fast as I can without showcasing my fear, trying to make it look more like a confident stride—regardless, I hope no one is around to witness it.

"Hey," a deep voice says from behind me, and I turn and press the button, a huge stream of pepper spray landing in his eyes. "Motherfucker. Why would you do that?"

I can barely make him out in the poorly lit parking lot, but then I do.

"Warner!"

"Yeah," he says, squatting on the ground, rubbing his face. "Shit, Gen."

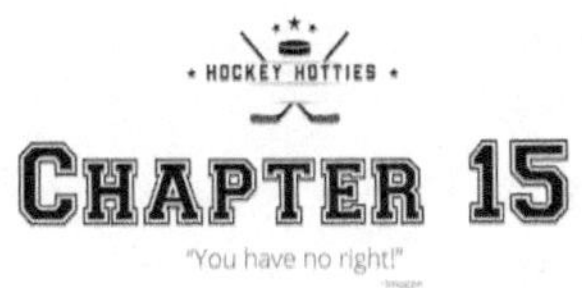

CHAPTER 15

Warner

My eyes burn as if there's a raging bonfire inside them, and I can't see shit.

"Why would you sneak up on me? You can't sneak up on a woman in a dark parking lot!"

I hear a car door open.

"Fuck. Get me to my car or something."

Nothing. Dead fucking silence until a car door shuts and I smell her perfume. "Open your eyes. I had a water bottle in the car."

She's in front of me now. I sense her there.

"I don't want to open my eyes. Do you have any idea how bad this fucking hurts?"

"Well... no, I've never been pepper sprayed."

I remove one hand and squint, but the pain is too intense, so I shut it immediately.

"Stop rubbing, it makes it worse. You have to open your eyes." Her hands are on me. Her delicate, silky soft hands are on me, and I wish I could enjoy the moment. The pinch of her perfect, manicured nails touches my eyelids. "Come on, Warner, I have to rinse it out."

"How do you know? Do you make a habit of macing people?"

She giggles, and her minty breath wafts under my

nostrils. How I've longed to have her this close to me, but not when I can't see her and not when I'm in this much fucking pain.

"No, but everyone knows you need to flush it out. Open up, big boy," she says, already pouring water on my face. Before I open my eyes fully, she uses two fingers and opens one for me.

"Thank God I don't wear contacts," I grumble.

"You should feel fortunate for that. Here it comes." A flush of water pours into my eye. "Now blink." She shifts her body to focus on the next eye.

I try to blink my eyes open, but damn, it still stings like a bitch. She does my other eye, then I no longer feel her presence and I hear her heels clicking away on the concrete. "Imogen!"

"I have to get more water. Just sit still."

"I'm in the middle of a parking lot and I can't see shit. I'm not going anywhere."

She chuckles. "It's kinda funny if you think about it. Of all the payback I envisioned over the years, I never came up with this. I think it's a really good one."

"What, did you plot my murder or something?" I fist my hands to stop myself from rubbing my eyes again.

"Shit. The door locked behind us." I hear her come closer and she slides her arm under mine. "Come on. I'll drop you off at a hospital."

"You cannot just drop me there when I can't see shit."

"Do you expect me to take you home?" She laughs and pushes me into her passenger seat. Just when I expect the door to close, her hair tickles my neck. "Time to get you all strapped in, little one."

The seat belt clicks into place and my hand falls over

hers to keep her close. Peeking through one eye, all I can see is her, but she's fuzzy with a halo around her.

"Please, Gen, I can't go to the hospital. The last thing I need to explain to anyone is why I was maced. Imagine the press."

She's so close, all I would have to do is inch forward and her sweet lips would be on mine. I wonder if she'd still be tentative, like our first kiss. I remember the first time I slid between her legs and told her over and over how much I loved her. Or has she grown up and, with more experience, is she confident in her skills as a lover? As much as I can't be upset if she is, I'd hate that another man got her to that point. That it wasn't me who taught her to trust her instincts and just feel.

She sighs. "I'll take you to Ford's."

My hand tightens around hers. "Gen, just take me to your house. We'll get my eyes flushed and I'll call an Uber."

She doesn't respond for a long time. "Okay." I can hear the hesitation in her voice.

"Thank you." I release her and her hair tickles me one more time before the door shuts.

Then she's in the driver's seat and she peels out of the parking lot.

"I can't believe you got me to agree to this," she says after a minute or so. "Do you know the lengths I've gone to so you wouldn't find out where I live?"

"Please, I've known where you live since the minute you bought the place."

"Ha, I didn't buy my place."

"Pretty sure you're the only Imogen Jacobs from New York in the vicinity. And you might not own it but you're renting it in your own name."

"Stalking is a crime, Warner." She turns and my body slams into the side of the car.

"So is murder." I readjust myself in my seat.

"If I wanted to murder you, I would've had it taken care of a decade ago." She slams on the brakes and I'm pretty sure the seat belt stops my forehead from hitting the window by a millimeter. It's hard to tell when I can barely open my eyes and they're watering so much.

"You love me too much to kill me."

"And what, you wanted to test that theory by doing what you did?" She presses hard on the gas, and I'm thrown back into the seat.

"I was young. I was stupid. When are you going to let me actually explain myself and not just say sorry?"

I glance at her and all I can make out is her head shaking back and forth. She's clearly upset. We should probably steer clear of this subject until we get to her house and she isn't behind the wheel.

"It's about character. You showed your true colors." She turns again, but this time my body goes in her direction. She knocks me with her arm, and I move back to my seat.

"Are you trying to kill us both by driving like this? We must be almost at your house by now. You don't live that far."

She verbally balks and I can't help but grin.

"Damn you! How did you find out?"

"I have my ways."

"Pervert," she whispers as the car comes to a stop. I think we're in her driveway, but neither of us attempts to get out of the car.

"Listen, I know you're pissed, but I really don't want to go blind right now."

"Always about you, isn't it?" She slams the door, then opens mine a few seconds later. "Let's go."

I fumble with my hands, but I manage to get out. I just don't want to open my eyes because that hurts the most. She leaves me to figure my own way up to her house. Since she's on the beach, I hear the waves washing up on shore.

"Come in," she says, but I put my hands out in front of me only for a door to shut in my face.

"Fuck!"

She opens the door again and takes my hand. "Whoops. Silly me. Looks like you dodged a bullet when you left me. I'd be a horrible caregiver when we're elderly."

"Somehow I doubt that," I mumble.

"Sit," she commands as if I'm a dog, pushing my shoulders down so my ass lands on a stool.

I turn my head in the direction I hear a faucet running.

"We do this, then you leave." She shoves an empty bowl against my chest. "Hold this."

I grasp both sides of the bowl.

"Open up, little baby," she says and hovers over me, forcing one eye open and pouring water into it.

I catch the water running down my face in the bowl. At least the best I can. She repeats the process with my other eye, then again with both.

I blink my eyes open and closed, finally able to see again. And it couldn't come at a better time because as Imogen steps back from me, I notice the water didn't just get into the bowl; it drenched her blouse. Her nipples poke through her bra and blouse and I have no control over my reaction. My dick goes full chub.

"Did you do that on purpose?" She yanks the bowl from me and the little amount of water that was in it splashes up onto her chest. I chuckle and she narrows her eyes at me. "Always games with you."

"That's unfair. I could barely see. I didn't purposely get your blouse wet." I stand and put my hands on the counter.

"Whatever. Don't you have an Uber to call now that you can see again?" She crosses her arms.

I try not to react to the visual of her wet tits wrapped in soaked silk. "I will, but we're going to settle this here and now. I'm tired of your attitude with me. Are you even listening to yourself? You called me a pervert and accused me of purposely trying to get your blouse wet. I'm not some thirteen-year-old boy. I can walk out that door and fuck any available woman I want."

A hollow, loud bark of laughter echoes through the empty house. "Then go. Why are you wasting all your time with me?"

"You know the answer to that. You're just refusing to actually listen to it. To believe it."

She rolls her eyes and looks at the wall. She's about to go into shutdown mode. I know it and I know I should back off. I have no right to ask her to sit here, dredge up the past, and cause her pain all over again. But damn it, I'm on my last thread and it's fraying like a knife is dragging back and forth across it.

She steps up to the counter on the other side of the island, both hands on the expensive stone, and leans forward. "Damn you. You know that? Damn. You."

"Why? Because I want you back?"

She stares at me, her breath quickening and her nostrils flaring. I'm surprised there's no smoke coming out of her ears. "You have no right!"

"I have every right because I fucking love you, Gen. I've always loved you. I'm not gonna hide in a corner forever. I fucked up. I know I did, and I deserved to be punished, but I've done my time. I'm here, asking you to give me another chance because I know what we had was special, and more than that, I know you know it too. Do you really think you'll be happy with anyone who's not me?"

She steps back from the counter, continuing until her back hits her fridge. "You asshole! You think you're so great. A great guy wouldn't ask the woman he loves to get rid of the child she's carrying!" A tear streams down her face and falls to the floor.

My fight dissolves into the ether as tears prick my eyes. "I was a child myself. All I saw was the weight of the responsibilities I already had to my mom and siblings. I wasn't like you, Gen. I didn't have everything money could buy."

She sinks to the floor and buries her head in her hands. I was naive to think we could get through this, because just hearing her say the words takes me right back there. To that moment when I first saw the same expression I do right now. The one that says the future between us has been ripped open by a butcher knife.

As I crawl onto the floor to join her, she lets me take her in my arms and hold her. If only the nightmare wouldn't plague me as well.

CHAPTER 16

Warner

So much had gone down at school. We'd lost the championship, and thanks to Peter, who'd done some digging, everyone at Lauder had found out I wasn't related in any way to Langley Wines. I'd pushed away all the shit people were saying about how Lauder had tried to buy the championship by giving an inner-city poor kid a scholarship, but that I wasn't good enough to get them one.

"Why didn't you tell me?" Ford asked one afternoon while he lay on his bed, tossing a hacky sack in the air and catching it. "I'm not like Peter or any of those guys."

When the news about my lack of lineage hit the rumor mill at school, I'd worried how Ford would react, but all I saw in his eyes was hurt. Ford had come to trust in our friendship, and I had deceived him twice. Once with Imogen and now with the fact that I was a nobody. Both times, he was awesome about it.

I stopped looking through the suits in his closet and sat on the edge of his king-size bed. "I don't know. The sick part is I think I enjoyed being someone else for a little bit. Not the poor kid without a future."

He stopped throwing the hacky sack and sat up. "You're joking, right? You're not nobody. You're gonna play for the Renegades." He pushed me with one arm. "Grab the navy suit. It's my best."

As if Ford couldn't have been a better friend already, he was letting me borrow a suit because the New York Renegades had asked me to come down and talk to their organization. With the draft only six weeks away, it was promising that a team was interested.

"I'd kill to be in your position, but we all know where I have to go."

"You act like going to college is a jail sentence." I glanced over my shoulder. "What if I get hurt in my first game?"

"You won't," Imogen said, walking into the room.

She looked off, but I knew she'd been taking some heat from some of the girls at school about me. Girls would approach me when she wasn't around and insinuate that they'd be a much more generous girlfriend. I wasn't stupid. Kids at school were under the impression that Imogen and I didn't have sex because I never mentioned it to anyone and neither did she. It wasn't anyone's business what we did or didn't do, and unlike most guys my age, I didn't see the need to advertise the fact that I was sleeping with the girl I loved.

"You can't be sure of that." I picked up the blue suit, but Imogen took it from me and hung it back on the rack.

"You look better in charcoal," she said.

"Hey, I picked the blue." Ford went back and lay on his bed, tossing the hacky sack in the air.

"You look good in blue because of your blond hair. Warner has darker hair." She ran her hands through my hair and stared up at me. Her eyes had a slight red-rimmed appearance, and I hated that she'd have to deal with all the bullshit at school on her own next year after I graduated.

I put my hands on her hips and drew her closer to me. "You okay?" I whispered.

She nodded and turned back to the suits.

"Rule one, you entered my room, which means you're on my time, sis," Ford reminded us.

I still kept my hands on her hips while she sorted through the suits. He and Imogen sometimes treated me like their favorite toy that their parents made them share. It felt as though one day my arm would be pulled from the socket. But I was happy because I wanted to spend all my free time with them.

"I have to find him a suit." She pulled one out and turned around, putting it up to my chest. I felt like a schmuck having to borrow from Ford. One day I'd have a huge closet full of suits and Imogen would have picked out every one for me. "This one is perfect."

I looked down and shrugged, taking it from her grasp. "Thanks." I kissed her cheek before heading into Ford's bathroom.

I heard mumbling behind the door while I changed, but I couldn't make out what they were saying. Graduation was in two weeks, and after the situation with Langley Wines, I was thankful to be able to hightail it out.

"What?" Ford's voice rose in volume, so I burst out the door with only the suit slacks on.

"What's going on?" I looked at Imogen, who was crying.

"Couldn't you keep it quiet for five minutes?" She stomped out of Ford's bedroom, and I heard her bedroom door slam.

"What happened?" I asked Ford. "Did someone do something to her?"

"You could say that." His expression was a mix of disbelief and concern.

"Whose ass do I have to kick?" I headed back to the bathroom to grab my clothes and the rest of the suit. "I'm going to go talk to her."

"Your own. You have to kick your own ass," he said, but I didn't comprehend what he was talking about as I walked out of his room. "This was my time!" he yelled.

I opened up Imogen's bedroom door and slid inside. After the Jacobs found out that Imogen and I were dating, they set a rule that I wasn't allowed in her bedroom. Luckily, they were up north with Morgan for her soccer tournament that weekend.

I glanced at my watch. I only had half an hour to spare, if that, before I needed to head to the Renegade stadium. Imogen had wanted to come with me and hang out until I finished, but I'd told her that was ridiculous. I'd just come back here, and we'd watch a movie since her parents were gone.

"Hey." I peeked my head through her door. "Can I come in?"

She took her pillow and plastered it to her face. "No. Just go get ready." Although her voice was muffled, I still heard her.

"I'm not going anywhere. What's going on? Someone being an asshole at school again?"

She shook her head.

I put my hand on the top of the pillow and lowered it. The fact that she allowed me to still surprises me today. Imogen wasn't a public person when it came to her feelings.

Tears ran down her face, so I slid onto the bed and leaned against the headboard, taking her in my arms. "Gen, what's wrong?"

She rose onto her knees and wrapped her arms around my shoulders, tugging on my naked flesh as if she was scared a monster would come and rip me away from her.

"Gen," I pleaded again, but her crying got worse.

"I'm... I'm pregnant," she wailed into my neck.

It was like everything came rushing at me at once. Visions of my mom not eating dinner so her kids could. Me as a child, crying because my dad had left and never returned. Someone in line behind us at the grocery store handing my mom ten dollars so she could afford the groceries she'd picked out.

I closed my eyes for a moment. We'd been so careful. Except that one time...

I drew back from our embrace so I could look at her. "How?" My voice sounded as raw as my emotions.

As soon as she wasn't buried in my neck, she hid her face from me, bringing up her hands. "I don't know. I've been late for a few weeks, but I thought it was stress. I Googled all these reasons, and it said that could be the cause of it. But I figured I better find out just in case. I thought for sure it would say negative and then once I wasn't stressing about my period coming, I'd get it."

I nodded, half in the room with her and half in my head, thinking of the ripple effect this would have on our lives. "Makes sense."

Moving as if she were sleepwalking, Imogen got off the bed and pulled a paper from her bag, handing it to me. Since my mom had been pregnant last year, I recognized it as an ultrasound photo. "But it didn't say negative. It said positive. I thought for sure it was wrong, so I went to the doctor and... what are we gonna do? I'm only a junior. I can't drop out. My parents are going to kill us. Ford is going to kill us."

I took her hands, finally seeing the front of the paper. An ultrasound photo. "We'll figure it out, but..." I looked from the photo to the clock. Time was going so fast. How could I handle this and get to the Renegades on time?

Her eyes narrowed on me a bit. "Figure what out? What do you mean?"

"Can we talk about this when I get back?"

She stared at me for an uncomfortable beat, then slid back from me. "Don't let me keep you."

"It's not that." I rushed to grab her hands, but she tore them away from me. "I'm just saying I have to go, and I'm in no mindset to make this decision right now."

"Make this decision? What are you implying?"

I stood, hurrying to put on the button-down shirt. "I'm just saying we're young. I'm about to embark on this hockey career.

We have plenty of time in the future to start a family, but... maybe not right now. We have options." I shook my head, unsure if even I could make sense of what I was saying. My thoughts were racing, and I wasn't even sure what I really meant.

Her hands flew to her stomach as though she felt she had to protect our baby from me. It felt like a stab to the heart.

"I didn't mean—"

"I heard you loud and clear."

"I don't know what I mean right now. I can't think straight. We'll talk about this tonight." I glanced at the clock again. Time was ticking away as though someone was moving the needle. "I have to go. I won't be able to support a baby if I don't get a spot on a team."

"Don't bother coming back tonight. I'm really tired."

"What?" My shoulders slumped, and I rushed to her. She wouldn't look at me though. "Come on, Gen. Don't be like that. I have to go. I'm sorry."

"Good luck. I hope you get everything you want." She rose on her tiptoes and kissed my cheek. "I love you."

"And I love you," I quickly said back because I did, but a baby? Fuck, a baby.

I'd seen my mom with Julien the past two years and it's a hard life. Especially if you're dirt poor. I didn't want to tell Imogen she didn't understand how much a baby would change our lives, but the reality was that she didn't. She'd been handed everything she'd ever wanted from the minute she was born.

"I'll be back, okay?" I ducked to look into her eyes, and after a minute, she nodded.

I sneaked one more kiss before leaving her room.

Once I was on the other side of her door, Ford came out of his room. He raised his eyebrows. "What's up, Daddy?" He ground out the words.

"We've used protection every time. How is this happening?" I pushed a hand through my hair.

"You couldn't keep little Warner out of my sister, that's how." I didn't hear anger there, but he was clearly upset.

"Take care of her until I get back?" I asked, hoping he would agree.

"Yeah. I will. Go. You're gonna be late."

I checked the watch Ford gave me so I looked the part. Damn it. I was going to be late. "I'm gone. Thanks again."

I jogged to the foyer and pressed the elevator button, feeling Ford's eyes on me. I felt like the biggest piece of shit having to leave at that moment, but I had no choice.

I hurried to press the first-floor button once I was inside the elevator. When I looked up, Ford was staring directly at me until the doors closed with a finality I wouldn't understand until later.

What did they think I could do? I needed the Renegades a helluva lot more than they needed me.

CHAPTER 17

Imogen

I pull my knees to my chest in an effort to not allow Warner to hug me, but he's stronger and I can't lie, his arms around me still bring a feeling of safety, even if I wish that weren't the case.

"Warner, we can't," I say, closing my eyes, wishing my words matched my actions.

"Just let me comfort you," he whispers, his head buried in my neck.

"I hate you."

"You don't hate me. Even if you wish you did."

More tears spill down my face, memories of the miscarriage forefront in my mind. I'd felt so alone in that hospital bed, and every time the hospital room door opened, I looked to see if it was him, but it never was. It had only been a day since I'd seen him and told him I was pregnant, but it felt as though a cavern had opened up between us because he wasn't there.

I push away from him and stand. "I do hate you. You left me. How could you just leave me there in a hospital all alone without any explanation?"

He stands too but doesn't come any closer to me. "You weren't alone. You had Ford. You had your family."

"I didn't have you!" I shout. "Why don't you understand that? To me, that room was empty without you."

"I went! I fucking went!" he blurts. I'm taken aback when a tear trickles down his cheek. "Did you think anything would've kept me from you?"

"Something did."

He grips his hair by the roots and nods. "I thought you wouldn't want me there. You were so mad about me wanting to discuss our options, but I went."

He's clearly holding something back, and if he thinks that after all this time we're going to move on from the past without him telling me the entire story, he is sorely mistaken.

"Then why did you never come in?"

He stares at the countertop, his finger following a dark line in the marble. "I don't want to start any more drama."

Fury hits me hard and fast. "Go, Warner." I point toward the door. "Just go!"

I head out the other door to the patio that overlooks the beach. My house is rented because I didn't know for sure whether this was just a pit stop or the final destination. I stand at the edge of my patio and stare at the dark ocean.

"The minute you called to tell me you were having a miscarriage, I came," he says softly from behind me, and I hear him step out onto the patio. "But when I arrived, Ford met me in the hallway."

I close my eyes and don't say anything.

"Do you remember that the McGregor brothers were failing Greek mythology senior year?" He stands beside me but keeps some distance between us, staring out at the same night sky. "Ford came up with a plan to steal the test and give them the answers so they'd pass."

I shake my head. "You guys are so stupid. Why would you do that?" I turn my head to look at him.

He shrugs. "Because we needed the win in the championship. The win would've brought scouts, and I needed to be drafted."

I don't see what this has to do with him abandoning me. "What does that have to do with you not being at the hospital?"

"Ford was pissed that I would even bring up the idea of an abortion. Looking back, I think he was also pissed that I was gonna be drafted, and he had to head to college to appease your father. I don't want to sound conceited, but he wanted the life I was about to have." A caustic laugh escapes him, and he shakes his head. "I also wonder if he was afraid he'd be pushed out of our lives if we had the baby. You know how sensitive he was about making sure he got his time with me."

I can't refute what he's saying. Ford was quick to anger when I told him that Warner was on the fence about keeping the baby. But he did make a few remarks about the two of us running off to live happily ever after if the baby was in our lives and he hadn't exactly sounded thrilled.

"I was young and stupid and scared shitless. Entering the draft was terrifying. What if no team wanted me? How would I ever help my mom? I couldn't afford college, and by that time, I'm not sure I could've found a school to give me a scholarship. Then you tell me you're pregnant and all I could think about was that I couldn't take any more pressure. I felt like I was being pulled in so many opposing directions. I couldn't have yet another person relying on me."

We're both silent for a beat.

"But I'm not proud of it, Gen."

"Can we please just stay on the Ford topic?"

He sighs. "He stopped me before I reached your room and told me I wasn't welcome. I thought he was just giving me hell, but when I went to sidestep around him, he blocked me. He threatened me."

I scoff. "Good to know it only took Ford blocking your way for you to abandon me."

"No, what I mean is he said that if I came near you, he'd tell the school I'd stolen the test. That I gave it to the McGregors. He went on about how he could get them to believe him because he's a Jacobs and I'm a nobody. That with his name came respect, but my name came with nothing. He only reconfirmed what I already knew to be true. The McGregors and a bunch of teammates would stay on Ford's side, I wouldn't graduate, the Renegades or any other team wouldn't want me, and I wouldn't be able to help my family. I'd be finished."

My voice breaks. "And you agreed?"

"What choice did I have?" he just about whispers.

"The honorable one. To honor the promise you gave me. Why is that so absurd?"

He breathes out a long stream of air and lowers his head. "You don't understand. The fact that I was even considering walking away from you convinced me that I wasn't good enough for you. I didn't fight. All I could think of was the responsibilities I had to my family, and I couldn't let them down. The minute I turned my back on you, the only way I got through these years was telling myself how you deserved much better than me."

I harden my voice. "And now?"

"I realize I was just a stupid kid. A child who didn't know how to handle an adult situation. All I saw was the money I could earn in the league and what my life and the lives of my siblings would be like if I didn't play professional sports. I didn't want Trinity or Julien to have to grow up worrying about where their next meal would come from or whether the landlord was going to kick them out in the middle of the night."

"It's always money to you."

"Because I didn't have any!" he shouts. "I didn't have *any*. And I'm sorry, Imogen, but you have no idea what that feels like or how desperate it can make you. I knew if I left you, you'd be okay. That your parents would always have a place for you. For me, it was either the draft or nothing."

"It didn't have to be that way. You were smart, Warner. You still are."

"By then I'd put all my eggs in the one basket. I saw one path out and that's all I focused on."

I can't deny he made it work. He might not have the money my parents do, or my siblings and me because of our trust funds, but he's a millionaire. And if I still know the real Warner, he's invested that money to make even more.

"Do you know how bad it hurts to know I wasn't enough to change your course?" I turn to face him, opening my soul.

He turns toward me. "I broke my heart too, Gen. Don't think I didn't. The only difference is you had hatred to keep you going all these years. I never stopped..."

"What?" I shake my head, confused.

"Loving you. I never stopped."

Hope and anger flare to life inside me. "Bullshit. I see the pictures." The words slip out of my mouth before I can think better of them. "You and Aria. You and other women."

"None of them have ever had a piece of me, Gen. It's only ever been you. Always."

Panic and self-preservation have me stepping off the deck onto the beach, wishing I would've cut off this conversation a long time ago. "I'm not sure what you want from me."

"A second chance. A date. Your heart."

"Is that the order?" I turn to face him, and he comes off the deck and steps closer, but I put my hand up to keep him back.

"I'll take you however I can get you."

I squeeze my eyes shut for a moment. I don't know what to do. I can feel myself getting sucked back in, even if my brain is screaming at me to run from the danger. But I cannot give him the ability to hurt me again the way he once did. Still, it's clear even to me that something is going to give. I just have to be the one in control of it this time.

"What if I suggested a fling? We get the sexual energy out of this equation. When I'm done with you, I toss you back into the dating pool?"

He laughs, then gives me that cocky, arrogant smirk. "You think it would be that easy?"

"I know it would. You might want to bare your soul to me, but I don't feel the same way." I cross my arms.

He steps closer, breaking the distance. "I think you're lying," he says in a low voice. "You forget I was there when we fell in love. One half of the equation. I can still feel it when we're in the same room."

I roll my eyes and huff.

"You think I'm wrong? The way you always dodge eye contact." His finger runs along my shoulder and down my arm, causing shivers to follow in its wake. "You can try to deny it, but you want me as much as I want you. There might be some physical need to it, but that's not all of it."

"You have no idea what you're talking about."

"Let me show you. Then I'll use the rest of my life making up the rest to you."

I let him open my arms, and he steps into me, his hands running along my neck, his thumbs gliding down the center of my throat. "How many times I've envisioned having you under me. My lips kissing every inch of your gorgeous skin. The way my name would come out of your lips as I thrust inside you. The begging, the pleading, the moaning..."

"Warner," I say it as an objection, but it sounds more like a plea and my eyes drift closed.

"I won't do anything else until you tell me to." He runs his thumbs over the column of my neck a little harder now. "Open your eyes, Gen."

I slowly do as he says and there he is. The first boy I ever loved. The only man I've loved. All I want to do is forget all the shit between us and let him take me. Skin to skin. Heartbeat to heartbeat.

"Tell me you want me, and you have me." He continues to rub his calloused fingers over my neck in what feels like the most divine torture.

I inhale, knowing the fight in me is over. Maybe I'm stupid, but I've always understood Warner. I don't like his explanation, but it doesn't mean I don't understand where it comes from. I came from so much privilege, and he didn't. Shame on my brother for using that against him. I'll deal with him later.

"Do you want me?" He draws me back to him. "Look at me."

My gaze slowly rises, and I quiver when our eyes lock. "Take me, Warner. Take me."

He doesn't wait a heartbeat before he steps closer to me, tilting my head up. His lips land on mine with determination and desire. My hands fly up to cover his, but he doesn't stop kissing me.

He strips his lips off of me. "We need to be alone for

what I have planned for you." He picks me up, so my legs are wrapped around his waist, and carries me back to the house. "Show me your bedroom."

We stop too many times to kiss again before we reach my bedroom. When we enter, he looks around the peach and bright-white decor that screams woman.

"You definitely need a little man in this room," he says.

"And let me guess, you're the little man?"

He chuckles and lowers me to the mattress, using his knee to widen my legs. "We both know there's nothing little about me."

"You cocky bas—"

His lips smash against mine, and my body relaxes as it finds its home again. All the nights I thought I'd never experience the euphoria of this moment, but here I am.

"Did you say something?" he draws back to ask.

I take him by his shirt and tug him back down. "Use that mouth for something better than talking."

He smiles and I melt into the mattress. "Yes, ma'am."

He falls on me and the weight of his body holding me down is the best damn feeling I've had since the last time I was with him.

CHAPTER 18

Imogen

Everything is way more intense than when we were younger. There's more rolling around, more fighting for dominance. More time spent on what comes before sex than the act itself. Which only leaves my whole body strung tight.

Warner is definitely taking the lead on this and I'm more than happy because his sole intention is to please me.

"Come here," he says, pulling me off the bed. "Stand." He positions me in front of him with his hands on my hips. I move to take off my high heels and his fingers dig into my hips. "Nope. Those stay."

"Did you get kinky in the past decade?" I ask, placing my hands on his shoulders.

"You've been tormenting me for weeks with these heels." His fingers touch the button on my slacks. "This okay?" he asks, looking at me.

I nod.

He stares at me the entire time he unbuttons my slacks and lowers the zipper. The tension in the room doubles as they fall down my legs and pool at my ankles. His vision shifts to my panties and his tongue slides over his bottom lip.

"You're so beautiful," he says softly, his fingers manipulating the bottom button on my blouse. "Tell me if this is too fast."

"I'm not seventeen, Warner," I remind him, although right now, it feels as if no time has passed.

"Definitely not." He shakes his head and continues to undress me. "Although I am disappointed that you lied. You said you didn't wear undergarments." He glances up with a smirk and it pulls a laugh out of me.

"That was that day. I guess you picked the wrong day."

"Oh... no. I picked the right day. Now I get to undress you."

He stands and pushes my blouse off my shoulders, and it floats down to the area rug. He holds his hand out for me and I accept it, stepping out of the pants.

"You have much more sophisticated panties and bras now." He toes out of his shoes, unbuckling his belt and unzipping his pants.

All I can do is watch in disbelief that I'm going to have him again. And a much more grown-up version of him, based on what I see already. He manages to strip himself down to only his boxer briefs so fast that I wish I'd done it myself, but I'm mesmerized by his body. The six-pack abs, the defined muscles where I don't remember him having muscles.

Going to the side of the bed, he situates himself to rest his back on the headboard and guides me to straddle him. I let my weight drop into his lap and his arousal grinds along my core, the panties and boxer briefs barely an obstacle.

He takes my head in his hands and places a sweet kiss on my lips. "Relax. It's just me."

A laugh bubbles up my throat and I have to pull my lips off his to let it escape.

"What?" The line on the bridge of his nose deepens.

"It's not *just you*. You're now Warner Langley, left wing for the Florida Fury. Mr. I Have My Whole Life Together."

That's not really what it is. It's that he's Warner. And though I tried to make this a fun romp in my head, there's always going to be an emotional weight to any intimate act between the two of us.

He tucks a strand of hair behind my ear. "Are you suggesting you preferred me when I was penniless and spineless?"

I shake my head and decide to be more honest. "You were the boy I loved, that's all."

He takes my hand and places it over his heart. It beats rapidly under my palm, as my own does. "And I still am."

I rest my forehead on his. We breathe the same air for a moment before he kisses my neck, causing a shiver to race up my back. His rough fingertips run down the length of my body and up my back, all while his lips explore my soft flesh. He undoes my bra and loosens the straps on my shoulders, slipping them down and revealing my breasts.

His eyelids grow heavier as his gaze skates over my bared flesh, then he sighs and positions me further up on him, palming my breast and bringing my nipple into his mouth. His tongue twirls and I clench below to keep my orgasm from building too fast. He mimics the action with the other breast, and I could fall apart in his arms. Never does he allow me to escape too far, his hands on me, sometimes a soft touch, other times a firm grasp. He still knows how to show his feelings with his body, because I haven't felt this loved since the last time I was in his arms.

I roll off his lap and he lies beside me so his face is at my stomach, hooking his fingers into the sides of my panties and sliding the fabric down while his mouth casts featherlight kisses against my stomach. His eyes search mine, and once he has my attention, he watches me while he situates himself between my thighs. He continues the sweet torment of soft kisses until he reaches my pussy. I wonder briefly whether he prefers me how I am today with just a landing strip. Back in high school, I was very *au naturel*.

My fingers grasp the comforter on either side of me when his tongue runs a circle over my clit. My hips buck up off the mattress.

"Shit," I whisper.

He chuckles into my pussy. "That's quite the reaction." He locks gazes with me again as he licks through my folds, sucking my hard nub into his mouth.

"Keep doing things like that and you're going to like the reactions you get," I pant.

"I don't plan on stopping. You know how committed I am when I want something." There's a spark of promise in his dark eyes.

The reference to how well I know him warms every inch of my body. It's as if he's telling me he hasn't changed over the years we've been apart.

He's a man of his word this time around, not using any fingers until I'm right on the brink of orgasm. He slowly pushes one digit inside, then two, arching them to hit my G-spot. I writhe under him, wet and out of control, trying to prevent my climax so that this moment doesn't have to end, but I'm desperate to ease the tension that's filled my body.

My orgasm washes over me like a wave that has me twisting and turning so I don't know which way is up.

"Ohhh..." My knuckles whiten where they grip the comforter tightly until my body has been wrung dry and I lie limp.

He slowly climbs back up my body, his hands running

the length of my sides, until our hands are clasped above my head.

"One," he says and kisses me.

I revel in the taste of myself on his tongue. I wiggle my body, desperate to touch him.

He chuckles and sits back on his ankles. "I hate to ask, but do you have condoms?"

I nod and open the drawer next to the dresser that also holds all my sex toys.

"Part of me hoped the answer would be no. I think I'd rather have blue balls than know you're readily able to fuck anyone else."

I get up on my knees and hand him the condom. He pulls off his boxer briefs, opens the package, and rolls it down his hard length.

"Sorry to disappoint you."

"You'll never disappoint me. It's my ego. But then again, after tonight, I'm hoping all those condoms are coming my way." He swoops an arm around my waist and pulls me into him. He's leaning back on his feet. "Straddle me."

I do as he says, thankful for the strength classes Lena's been demanding I do with her.

He positions himself at my center and I sink down on him slowly, feeling myself stretch around his girth. We both swear once I'm fully seated on him and he fills me. Another part of his body that has grown since our teenage years, I'm sure of it.

His rough palms graze my hips, running up and down, and he pulls me up by the waist a bit and draws himself out of me from below. Then he surprises me and thrusts into me with force. I cling to his shoulders, and he tightens his arms around me, continuing to move in and out of me at a steady pace.

"I've missed you," I say, unable to keep the words to myself.

"I'm nothing without you in my life. I'm so sorry I was an asshole. I never should've stayed away this long." He grips me tighter, as though he's afraid I'll disappear.

Then he forces me away from him, so my shoulders and head are back on the bed, and he kneels in front of me, holding my pelvis up to him by the waist while he moves in and out of me. He watches our joining with avid interest and licks his lips.

"You're so fucking beautiful, Gen."

"Warner, I—" My words fade away as I lose any rational thought and moan.

The man has my climax on a tightrope, and with each move, I think he's going to let me free-fall before the net catches me, but no, he changes it up right before I'm there. He brings me closer to him again and my hands are on his shoulders while I drive myself up and down on his steel length.

His thumb runs the length of my lips, dips into my mouth, and runs over my lips again. "I love your lips."

"I love everything about you," I confess, my body ready to give up its second orgasm.

"Me too, but I love your lips most when you're pissed at me. It makes me want to kiss them and make you surrender to me."

"Surrender? Don't make me lose my impending orgasm, Mr. Langley."

He gets me on my back in the missionary position before I can blink. "I like that Mister stuff. It's like you're giving me authority over you." He pushes back into me with a moan that vibrates in his chest.

"Don't count on it in the future."

He circles his hips, and that's it. One more surprise move of his and it's game over for me.

"I'm starting to think I like to hate fuck. You turned me on with your venom these past few weeks."

I bring my legs up and dig the heels of my designer shoes into his ass cheeks. "Is this what you envisioned?"

He thrusts deeper and I groan from the pleasure.

"Again," he says.

I dig the ends of my heels into his ass again and he pounds into me.

"Free your calendar tomorrow."

"Why?"

He gets up on his elbows and looks at me. "Because you're busy. Clothing optional."

Just the thought of spending a naked day with Warner makes my climax impossible to hold back.

He kisses my neck. "Just let go. I've got you."

And he does. Except that one time. And I have to decide if I'm willing to chance it happening again because being here beneath him, I know all the feelings I've ever had for him are still there.

I come on a strangled cry, back arching off the bed.

"I love you, Gen," he breathes into my ear. "So fucking much."

He makes the shift between sex to lovemaking seamlessly as his movements slow and he whispers his love for me over and over until he stills inside me with a guttural moan. Without moving, he kisses under my earlobe.

"And it wasn't the sex that made me say I love you," he whispers. "I want you to be mine. Tell me you forgive me?"

I didn't think he'd ask what this means so fast, but he gets up on his elbows and stares at me, waiting for my answer.

I'd be kidding myself if I said I didn't feel better about what went down all those years ago now that I know the whole story.

"I forgive you," I say, and a huge smile creases his lips.

But just because I forgive him doesn't mean I have to let my guard down yet. He surprised me once and I won't let him do it again. I like to think I don't repeat my mistakes.

CHAPTER 19

"No secrets."
—Warner

Warner

After I've disposed of the condom in the bathroom, I place my hands on the counter and lean in to look at myself in the mirror. "You've got her back. Don't screw it up this time, asshole," I mutter to myself.

I meant what I told Gen. I'm going to do whatever it takes for her to understand how devoted I am to her. But there's a niggling worry at the back of my mind that I'm finally poised to get everything I ever wanted, and fate might step in and steal it from my grasp.

I enter the bedroom where Imogen is lounging on the bed in a postorgasmic glow. Jesus, I'm undeserving of her.

"I couldn't help but notice that in the drawer with the condoms..." I begin to open the drawer and Imogen flies over from the other side of the bed and slams it shut. "Sorry, babe, I've already seen it all."

I sit on the edge of the bed, blocking her access, and open the drawer again. She crawls up my back, reaching forward, but we both know she can't get through me. I pick up the closest vibrator wrapped in a velvet pouch. Only Imogen would neatly put away all her sex toys. I shut the drawer and move so my back rests against the headboard.

"What's behind door number one?" I eye her as I untie the strings.

She's on her knees with her head in her hands. "I can't believe you're doing this."

I chuckle. "When did you start going into sex toy shops?"

"Give me a break. I order online like everyone."

I fiddle with the purple vibrator. At least there's no ego crush on the size. "What does this one do? I assume this is for the clit?" I thumb the smaller part that looks as though it has a small suction hole.

"You know what it does." She goes to her side of the bed.

"Why don't you demonstrate for me?" I hand it to her.

"I'm exhausted," she says, turning to face away from me.

"Then I'll use it on you." I run my palm between her legs, opening her for me.

She happily obliges and turns onto her back, her legs spread open. I reach into the drawer for some lube and put it on the larger, curved portion.

"Do you prefer this over me?" I inch the tip in and press a button, not sure what it does.

"It was your replacement. And he doesn't talk during the sex, so I do quite enjoy him."

"Him, huh? Does he have a name?" I arch an eyebrow.

She bites her lip, and I bend down, using my teeth to release her bottom lip.

"Tell me," I whisper.

She wiggles on the bed as I push it farther inside her. "Bentley," she says.

"Bentley? What can this thing do?" I press another button and a sucking sound comes from the smaller part wand, so I angle it over her clit. Her back arches off the mattress. "Is this why its name is Bentley?"

"Partly. It can replace any man."

I bend down again, careful not to touch her. Once she's right under me, I whisper, "Do you still believe that?"

She shrugs. "I've only seen one of your moves so far. The verdict is still out."

I laugh and press another button to increase the intensity of the vibrations. Her breasts rise and fall, and I love the reactions I'm pulling out of her.

I slide the vibrator out and slowly slide it back in. "What else does this thing do?"

"It heats up," she says, probably because she wants me to use that feature. I'm not sure if I want to continue to tease her or just let her have her orgasm.

Finding another little button, I click it on. Judging by Imogen's reaction, I'd say I hit the right one. Her hands float over her body until they each land on a breast. They squeeze and tweak and squeeze again. I watch her getting off on the vibrator buried in her pussy with her hands on her tits.

"God, I wish I could film you," I say and her eyes snap open, her palms pressing down on the mattress. "But I'm not."

She relaxes again, and it doesn't take long to get her back to that euphoric state. Moans echo through the room and her body slides along the sheets, her tits raising up, tempting me to take one in my mouth, but I want her to enjoy this without my hands or mouth. All I'm doing is manipulating the instrument inside her that's doing all the work.

Her breath comes in short, steady spurts, signaling that she's growing closer, so I press the button to increase to the maximum vibration.

Her hand shoots out. "No, go back."

I switch the vibration back to where it was, and she eases back down to the mattress with a sigh. She's the complete opposite of the teenage girl I used to sleep with. Young

Imogen was shy and never wanted to tell me what she needed to get off. I'm one hundred percent sure she faked orgasms in the beginning. Until I got the hang of how to please her.

She brings her hips off the bed, pushing her pussy in my direction, wanting the vibrator to go deeper. Although I want to tease her, I push the vibrator as far as it will go. Hovering over her, I allow my lips to taste her breath, but that's all.

"Get inside of me," she says.

I shake my head. "You've got Bentley."

"Jesus, Warner, if I wasn't a second from coming, I'd refuse to give you the pleas—"

I increase the suction on her clit, and she can't finish the sentence.

"Shit, I'm coming, and it feels fucking amazing." Her body tenses, and for a moment, I wonder if she's going to allow the tension to leave her body. She jerks and a small smile creases her lips as she moans, then goes limp.

"I love watching you come."

She squirms to get the vibrator out of her with my help. "I can't believe I just did that."

"Technically, I did all the work. You just lay there and got off."

She playfully smacks me, and I toss the vibrator on her side table and take her in my arms. Her skin is so soft, I could stay in bed with her day and night.

"Warner," she says a second later in a tone too serious for my liking.

"What?"

"We'll have to tell Ford."

I kiss her shoulder. "I'll take care of it. Don't worry."

She circles in my arms and shakes her head. "No. I'll tell

him. We have some other things to discuss." Her voice isn't pleased, and I know she's going to give her brother hell for what he did at the hospital. I wonder if that will make it more difficult for him and me to find common ground. "But I want to keep this between us for a while."

I blow out a breath. I don't want a repeat of high school.

I open my mouth, but she places her finger over my lips. "Listen, this is new, and I'm afraid if we tell Ford, he'll tell my parents, and the pressure from all sides would just be too much. They'd have questions and their own opinions of the two of us. I'm only asking for a few weeks to enjoy this and make sure we have an honest shot at a relationship."

"I don't like secrets. It feels like lying."

She nods. "I know, and it won't be long. Just so we can enjoy one another like any other couple would when they start dating." She places her hands on my cheeks. "Don't you think we deserve that? After all we've been through?"

I nod. "But not long."

"I promise." She inches closer and kisses me. "You're okay with that?"

I'm not sure how she expects me to answer, but I can be patient until Imogen is convinced I'm the one for her. "Sure."

"Thanks." She gives me a soft smile. One I've been waiting to see aimed at me for damn near a decade. "Now I feel kind of dirty. You want to clean me up?" She gets off the bed and offers me her hand.

"Nothing would give me more pleasure, unless you want me to clean you up with my tongue while we're in there," I say, completely joking, but she palms my dick.

We make our way to the shower, and she turns on the water and grabs two towels while the water is warming.

Imogen's place consists of light colors, very clean and organized. Not that I expected any different.

"You know your plan has a hitch," I say as she busies getting her things together for after the shower.

"What's that?"

"If we're a secret, you can't sit in the wives and girlfriends' section, and you can't wear my number. Did you know the guys have a competition on how to bling out their wives and girlfriends?"

She laughs. "Yeah, Ford bought Lena the most gaudy diamond necklace with his number on it. Annabelle almost cracked her first tooth on it, so that's back in a jewelry box now."

"Damn it, he took my idea." I laugh because all I care about is that she wears my jersey. I don't need to involve myself in the other guys' plans. I just want to see number thirty-four on Imogen's back again. I'll make sure to palm the camera guy some extra money to get that on camera.

"I feel bad for the wives and girlfriends. Those guys buy the worst items. Especially Maksim." She wraps her arms around my neck, pressing her naked body to mine. "I promise I'll make it up to you."

I smack her ass and smooth my hand over her now pink flesh. "You better." I laugh to let her know I was joking.

"Do we need to talk about kinks? First sex toys, now ass smacking." She smiles and leads me into the shower.

"Ouch!" I shout and step back from the stream of water. "Holy shit, are we trying to burn away our sins?"

She stands under the water, and I see her pale skin grow pinker and pinker. "Aren't you the tough hockey player? It's just hot water."

"I'm not a lobster that needs boiling."

She rolls her eyes and adjusts the heat. "Noted. You're a baby when it comes to water temperature."

I pick her up and step under the stream of water. "You think you're so funny."

I bend down and kiss her neck. Her thighs tighten. I could take her again right here and now, but the condoms are in the other room.

"There is one thing I need to know before we move forward?" she says and I place her down before squirting shampoo into my palm. "No secrets, right?"

I pause from the concern laced in her voice. "No secrets."

"Who is Iris?"

"Ah, the whole reason I followed you tonight." I bring my hands up to her head.

"Followed?"

I massage the shampoo into her hair, and she turns and leans back, her hands on my outer thighs. "I told the guys I'd meet them at Carmelo's because I wanted to straighten you out and wait for you to say you were sorry."

She tries to look back, but I keep her facing forward. "You're unbelievable."

"Do you want to guess who Iris is?"

"No."

"Are you sure? You seemed kind of annoyed when you had my phone and she called. We could make a game of it?"

"Warner..."

I chuckle. "Okay, she runs my nonprofit. It's back where I was playing before, but I want to open a branch here. I haven't been able to visit the other one and the kids are used to seeing me."

She turns in my arms, suds of shampoo piled high on her head. "What is it? I didn't have you listed as having a charity when I got your paperwork."

"Because I don't publicize it. It's something I do for the kids. I don't need any praise for doing it." I pause because I've only trusted a few player friends and my family with this information. "We buy sports equipment for underprivileged kids. I have a few teams too, but mostly I focus on equipment."

She places her hands on my chest. "Warner." She kisses my chest. "You do it because—"

"I know what it's like not to have what you need. What everyone else has. Sports are all about confidence. How can you be confident when the kid next to you has state-of-the-art shit and you've got rusty skates that your mom's friend got from a friend of a friend whose son played once upon a time?"

She nods because she might not understand exactly, but Imogen has a huge amount of empathy for people. That's one of the many reasons I fell in love with her.

"Do you want to go sometime?" I ask and hold my breath for her answer.

"I'd love to."

I bend down and kiss her, which turns more intense quickly.

"Warner," she says when I strip my lips off of hers to explore her body.

"Uh-huh?"

"The shampoo is burning my eyes."

"Oh, yeah."

We both laugh and have her step into the stream of the water, allowing the suds to travel down the length of her mouthwatering body. If I'm able to keep her this time around, I really am the luckiest bastard in the world.

CHAPTER 20

Imogen

"**W**ell, I'd say we used that forty-eight hours well." Warner wraps his arms around my waist and tugs me toward him. He's wearing his slacks, no belt, and his shirt only has a few buttons done up.

"Agreed." I'm not sure I've had that many orgasms in that short of time before. And as much as I'm not ready to say goodbye to him, I need some space. He cannot be my entire world the way he was when I was a teenager.

"Hey, so…"

I hate when he starts a conversation like that. It means he's uncomfortable, which makes me anxious.

"Aiden Drake asked me to a dinner party at his place next month."

"You can't go." The words fly out of my mouth in a knee-jerk reaction. Aiden means Ford.

He chuckles. "Aiden's pretty set on me going. He wants to be the Band-Aid for Ford and me."

"Did you tell him even super glue isn't going to fix things between you two?"

He releases me and goes to the kitchen counter where his wallet and keys are. "You should know that I want to fix things with Ford too. I have to. The team is suffering because of our dynamic."

I look at the floor and back at him. "I know. I see it."

Everyone does. The announcers and analysts have started saying that Mr. Gerhardt made a mistake bringing on Warner. Whatever the reason they hate one another, it obviously can't be resolved. I'd never tell Warner that I overheard Mr. Gerhardt at a recent game saying one of them might have to be traded. If it's Ford, he'll leave as quietly as a bear leaving a campsite. And if it's Warner... well, I don't even want to think about how I might feel about that.

"Anyway, I decided I'm going. Were you invited?"

I nod. "I was."

"Do you think there's a chance we might be out by then?"

"Me and you?"

He nods with a cocky, lopsided grin. "Yeah."

"I don't know. But that brings up something else I wanted to talk about."

He shifts his weight. "Should I sit back down?"

I laugh. "No, because we both know what's going to happen if you sit down."

"I know what I *want* to happen if I sit down. Hell, even if I'm standing here truthfully."

I wait a second until I have his full attention. "I love what we've done these past two days, and I don't regret it, but... I want us to date too?"

He walks over to me and cages me against the counter, both hands on either side of my body, leaning forward. "Are you asking me to date you in secret?"

I nod.

"You know what that means though?"

"What?"

"I can't wine and dine you. At least not publicly. We'll have to sneak around. You sure you're okay with that?"

I'm not sure of the answer he wants, but I know the answer I have to give. "We did it once. We can do it again."

"All right, but be prepared, because this time, I'm not a poor high school student."

"Is that a warning?" I put my hands on his shoulders and use them as leverage so I'm sitting on the counter.

He expertly wiggles his hips between my legs and pulls me so my ass is practically hanging off the counter. "I'm going to make you wish you could Instagram it or TikTok the living shit out of what I'm gonna do for you."

My fingers play with the hair at the back of his head, and he draws closer. "Is that a promise?"

"It's a pinkie promise."

Our lips touch and his tongue slides into my welcoming mouth. I really don't want him to go, but we need some distance. At least I do right now. Just to put my feelings in order.

"I'll see you soon," I murmur against his lips.

He picks me up by my hips and places my feet on the floor. "Since you're so hell-bent I leave, show me the way."

I step in front of him and walk to the door. I'd love to tell him to stay, but I was that girl who made a boy her entire world once upon a time and it didn't work out well. This time I need to be sure to have a better balance.

Once we reach my front door, I open it and step aside to let him leave.

"So, this is it?" he asks. I roll my eyes and he laughs. "I'll see you tonight at the game, right?"

"I'll be there, and those boys will be too. First row just left of the goal."

"You're sitting with them?"

I shake my head.

"Where then?"

"In the wives and girlfriends' section."

He grins, and it lights up his dark eyes from within. "Does that mean I can buy you my jersey?"

I place my hand on his hard chest. "It means I'm helping Lena watch Annabelle."

"Well, keep an eye on number thirty-four. I heard that he's got an awesome backhand."

"Eh... he's mediocre at best." I wink.

Warner tickles my ribcage. "Mediocre, huh?"

"He is seeing a really hot number on the side, though," I say through my laughter.

His fingers tickle me until he gets me against the door-jamb. "I love you."

I run my hands down his chest and my stomach flips. "I love you too."

"Amazing how fast we got back here." He kisses my forehead, my nose, then my mouth. "See you tonight."

"See you tonight. Get some rest before the game!" I call.

He laughs and puts his hand in the air, climbing into the Uber that's been waiting patiently.

God, the man oozes sex appeal. I'm sad to see him go, but proud of myself for taking the space I know I need.

THAT NIGHT, I'm headed to the locker room to tell Warner that his special guests are here when I run smack-dab into Ford.

"What are you doing back here?" he asks. He's wearing his suit still, which means he didn't do warm-ups.

"What's wrong?" I eye his suit in case he wonders how I would know.

"Ah." His hand goes to the back of his neck, and he pulls.

"Annabelle has a fever. I wasn't going to be here, but Lena told me that I have to trust her. And it's not like I don't, it's just—"

"You want the control of being there."

He balks. "That's what Lena said. And it's not true. I don't see the harm in me wanting to be there when my daughter is sick." He slides past me. "I gotta go."

"Can you send Warner out?"

His feet skid to a stop right outside the doors. He doesn't turn around but does a dramatic pause before looking at me over his shoulder. "Why?"

"Because he offered some tickets to a group of boys and they're here. I just wanted to let him know where they're sitting."

"I'll send him out." He doesn't say anything else before pushing through the doors.

I lean my back against the wall opposite the doors and wait.

"Is that *the* Imogen Jacobs? The woman who left my office a couple days ago and I haven't heard from since? The same woman who was seen on the security cameras putting her ex-boyfriend in her car?" Jana laughs as she walks toward me.

"You're kidding me," I whisper-shout.

She shakes her head. "Why are you standing out here?"

"Because it's the locker room," I say quickly before changing the subject. "How many people saw us in the parking lot?"

"No one. Well, me and Fred." She steps across the hall, one hand on the locker room door.

"Jana, they could be naked in there."

She looks at me over her shoulder. "One can only hope. Let's go."

I follow her, half closing my eyes and half trying to make sure I don't run into a wall.

"By the way, I expect details," she says.

"It was dreadful. I maced the man."

She chuckles and stops to turn and look at me. "I know. That's why I want details." She spins back around and steps farther in. "Heads up, boys. There are some ladies in the house."

"Miss Gerhardt, this is a men's locker room," Coach Vittner says, coming out of his office.

"Sorry, but we have some business to attend to. Warner." She snaps her fingers and nods in my direction. "Imogen needs you."

"Jana, what the fuck are you doing?" Kane approaches her, wearing only his jockstrap.

My eyes bulge out, but Jana crosses her arms and doesn't let her eyes roam from his face. My hero, I tell you.

"I'm simply conducting business. If I had to wait around for you all to be dressed, I'd get nothing done."

"You can't be here."

Jana sticks out her arms and glances across the room. "Anyone besides Kane Burrows have a problem with me being here?"

Everyone says no.

"Like they're going to say yes." Kane dips his head and leans into her a bit. "This isn't ethical."

"I'm not ogling anyone. I'm here to talk to Coach Vittner."

"Then come into my office," Coach says with a sharp tone. Probably upset she's bothering his players before a game.

"What's up?" Warner surprises me, and I shake my head to clear it.

"I was going to wait outside."

"I'd prefer that, but do what you want. None of these boys have what I do," he says in a low voice.

I can't fight off my smile, no matter how hard I try to think of anything else.

"Hold up and I'll come with you two." Ford barely has one skate on and only one arm is through his jersey.

The two of us look at him.

"We got it," I say, putting my hand in the air before I lead the way for Warner to follow.

Once we're in the hallway, some other staff are still coming and going in and out of the locker room. I can hear the crowd in their seats, waiting for the game to start.

"I just wanted to let you know that the boys are a little left of the goalie. You should spot the red-haired one."

"You told me this already. Are you sure..." He looks both ways down the hall. "You're not just here to give me some good luck before the game?"

"No." Okay, maybe a little. "The red-haired kid's name is Braydon. Then you have Hayden and Layton. The mom is Carrie, and she brought a friend, Penelope."

He's nodding but paying no attention. Instead, he walks down the hall away from the locker room.

"I need to go find my seat. Lena isn't coming tonight. Annabelle is sick." I quickly follow him.

"Still sit in the wives and girlfriends' area. I'm prepared to see you there after I score." He winks. Oh, the ego on this man.

He stops when he reaches a door, then opens it and waits for me to go in first. It's a storage room filled with cleaning supplies.

I take a hesitant step inside. "How romantic. Are we going to role play Cinderella and the prince?"

Warner wastes no time following me inside. He flicks the lock, and his lips are on mine. "God, I missed you and it's only been hours. Tell me you'll come home with me tonight. I promise to make it worth it." His hands slide around me and grabbed my ass cheeks. But his pads take up so much room that I can't get as close to him as I want.

I slide my tongue into his mouth, and the way his hand holds the back of my head and he angles us the perfect way tells me he likes the initiative I took. He groans, and I want to jump in his arms and tell him to play with me attached to him, that I never want to let him go, but that was the needy girl in high school. So I step back and wipe my lipstick from his lips with my thumb.

"Good luck out there." There's a breathy quality to my voice.

"One more?"

I hear the guys coming out of the locker room, doing the stick-tapping thing they always seem to do. Kane's deep voice barrels through the small space with some motivational words for the team.

"Where the hell is Langley?" someone asks.

But the roar of Coach coming out thankfully diverts their concern, then it's a stampede of men down the hallway toward the ice.

"After the game, I'll text you my address." His eyes are filled with hope.

"We'll see."

"Okay." He nods, and I assume he doesn't want to rush me.

He peeks out of the door and slams it shut.

"Peekaboo!" Jana yells from the other side as she opens the door, finding the two of us in the storage closet. "Thinking about taking up another position in here?" She laughs. "Say goodbye to your heartthrob and let's go find some seats," she says to me, then turns her attention to him. "Bye, Warner, good luck."

"Yeah, bye." He heads out.

"Don't forget to give a wave to the boys," I call.

"Sure thing." He nods.

Jana continues to laugh through the uncomfortableness of the moment.

Once Warner is out of sight, I stare her down like I would a good friend. "You couldn't have just left and let us remain a secret?"

"Where's the fun in that? Do you know what a boring life I lead? I have to live vicariously." She slides her arm through mine as she often does and leads me to the ice.

At least it was Jana and not Ford.

CHAPTER 21

"Imogen Jacobs, get out of my locker room!"
—Coach Vézina

Warner

I skate onto the ice and Drake comes to my side immediately. "What are you trying to do, ruin your chances of us winning the Cup?" His voice is low, and he keeps looking around.

"What are you talking about?"

"The fact that you and Imogen weren't in the hallway when the team went out. And you just got here now. Do you think Ford hasn't noticed?"

"Nothing's going on. It was just about some kids I got tickets for." I look over to where Imogen told me they'd be and give them a nod. They wave and I return the gesture.

"I'm just saying, I'm trying everything to get us going as a team and the last thing we need is you and Imogen replaying a take two of whatever the fuck happened in high school."

I pat his shoulder. "Relax, it's all good."

I skate off so I don't have to lie anymore. I've come to like Drake since being with the Fury and I'd hate to put him in a shitty situation. Especially since he's trying to get Ford and me to reconcile our friendship.

Midway through the game, neither team has scored. Drake's tried a bunch of times, as have I, but Ford's been all over the place. When Drake shoots Ford the puck and he loses it within a second, our captain's frustration turns to anger.

"Get your fucking head in the game or get off the fucking ice!" Drake shouts at Ford.

"It wasn't my fault. That was a shitty pass."

I skate between them to keep them away from one another. "Anyone want to help me get the fucking puck back?"

"Stay out of this, Langley," Ford says, but skates like he's chasing me away from his sister down to the other side of the ice.

Maksim throws his body into another guy and gets a hold of the puck, passing it back to Drake.

The kids who came to see the game all have wide eyes since it happened right in front of them.

"Meet you at the usual place." Drake winks at me and skates like hell.

It's all I can do to catch up to the guy, but I do, and right before he circles the net, Drake passes the puck to me and I slapshot the puck toward the net. The buzzer sounds and the light glows red. All our arms fly up. Well, all but Ford's.

After the celebration, we all realize that Ford's about to go a few rounds with Nashville's defender, Ricky Whirly.

"I'm not sure why you're starting shit tonight, Richie. Did your wife leave you? Or worse, is she fucking Langley?" Whirly laughs.

Aiden and I look at one another, knowing this isn't going to end well.

"This has nothing to do with my wife." Ford throws his gloves on the ice and the crowd cheers.

The refs are there, but they hang back, waiting to see

what's going to happen. Sometimes you gotta let the guys get a few punches in before you break it up.

"Stop being an asshole!" Maksim screams, coming to our side to watch what's gonna happen. It's a little ironic, given that he had some anger issues on the ice before I was traded to the team.

"Shut up. You assholes love Langley so much, have him take my spot," Ford says.

"Your spot?" Aiden shouts over the crowd.

"You really want this, huh?" Whirly says. "All right, you got yourself a fight. For your sake, I hope your wife is home to play nursemaid when I'm all done with yah." Whirly's gloves hit the ice and they circle each other.

"We're not chicks and our friendship isn't exclusive," Maksim shouts, elbowing Aiden.

"Just hit the fucker so we can all get on with the game!" Tweetie yells from the bench.

I glance at the wives and girlfriends' area and spot Imogen standing to get the best view she can.

"Aiden loves Langley. You guys were on my side and now he's shifting. Constantly chirping in my ear about passing Langley the puck and shit." As Ford circles Whirly, he's busy talking to his friends.

"Maybe I should go," I say like the mistress.

"What about me? You fuckers leave me out all the time. I'm off the starting line! Do you see me crying?" Tweetie chimes in from the bench again.

Kane skates over and takes off his goalie mask. "If you want therapy, go see Maksim's girl. This whole thing is bullshit!"

"Sounds like you have issues that don't involve me," Whirly says.

"You've been playing dirty all night," Ford says. "This is me and you."

"You sure? Maybe you want to go home and tell Mommy that your friends are all being mean to you?" Whirly raises his eyebrows.

The referee skates closer to the outside of their circle. "If fists don't get involved in a minute, I'm gonna blow this whistle and you both go to the box anyway."

"Let's go." Ford circles again and grabs Whirly by the jersey to keep him steady, cocking his other arm back and throwing the first punch.

"Finally, at least they're fighting. About what? Who knows." Aiden rests his chin on the edge of his stick, and we watch.

"I saw Whirly do some dirty shit, but he usually keeps it in check unless it's Langley." Maksim throws a nod in my direction.

"He probably wishes it was me." I glance back up at Imogen.

"It's a classic case of transferring."

Aiden, Kane, and I look at Maksim.

"Is that what does it for your girl? You say a few psychology words and she gets all hot?" Kane says.

Maksim looks at Kane. "Unless you want us to be the next two fighting, leave my girl out of this."

Kane holds up his big gloves. "Not judging, but whether it's transferring or whatever, you better get your boy in line. I didn't come to the Fury to keep losing."

He skates off toward the goal and sips from the water bottle he keeps on top of the net.

Ford can fight, so I'm not surprised when Ford gets Whirly on the ice and the ref blows his whistle, calling the fight. Ford heads to one penalty box and Whirly to the other.

I look back up at the stands and Imogen is no longer there.

The game starts again, and Train subs in for Ford, expertly playing with us and scoring the next goal. He does his usual celebration of a train whistle and his arm pumping up and down in the air.

The crowd goes crazy. Coach takes our line out and we head back to the bench. Ford is still pouting in the box, but I do a double take when I spot Imogen on the other side of the glass. She's telling him something and he's rolling his eyes.

"They're close, huh?" Drake asks me.

"Since he's hated me for ten years because of what I did to her, I'd say they're pretty damn close." I laugh, although it isn't funny.

"Is he that worried about losing me as a friend? I have to say I feel honored." Drake squirts some water into his mouth.

Maksim leans forward. "Don't be honored. It's him being protective of Langley."

My face screws up. "What? He hates me."

"Maybe, but if he can't have you, nobody can."

I look back over at Ford in the penalty box. Imogen's throwing her hands in the air and stomping away. That might just hit the highlight reel tonight.

"Yeah, I don't think that's it," I say.

"Think about it." Maksim makes Superstar move over on the bench so he can get next to Drake. "You and he were like some dynamic duo back in high school, right?"

I nod.

"And now you and Aiden are." He raises his eyebrows.

"I'm going on record as saying you're spending way too much time with Paisley. Next thing we know, we'll see Maksim Petrov, MD, on the door upstairs." Aiden laughs, and the whistle blows.

We file back out onto the ice and Ford gets out of the sin bin. The whole time, all I can think about is what Maksim said. Could he be right?

I know Ford hates me, but I figured he didn't like me working with Drake because that was his best friend. But he was protective of me when we were younger, and Ford likes to keep his friends close. No way Maksim is right though. Him not wanting Drake and me to be the new dynamic duo on the ice isn't why he's so pissed. Even if our friendship did end abruptly.

WE WIN THREE TO ONE, and the second we're in the locker room, Coach says, "Jacobs, my office. Now." He slams the door shut after Ford enters.

We all know why he's getting called in, so even though we won, everyone goes to the showers with little fanfare.

"What was all that about on the ice?" Cory asks me.

I feel for the kid. He's a rookie in the league, he's new to the team, and when you aren't playing all the time, you can feel left out. For that reason, I hated my first two seasons with a vengeance.

"Ford's just going through menopause," Train says and heads to the opposite side of the showers.

"Something must've happened at home. Lena and Annabelle weren't at the game, which is unusual." I don't want to say that Imogen told me Annabelle is sick. The less attention I can draw to the two of us, the better.

"I always find it hard to keep my mind on the game when something is going on at home."

"That's where I'm different. For me, the ice is a distraction," Kane says, rubbing shampoo through his chin-length hair.

"Did you ever wonder if that's because you're single? Like if you settled down, maybe you wouldn't be able to shut out the real world?" Cory asks.

"Two therapists on this team now, eh?" Kane says. "Take it from a veteran. Once you get on the ice, push all that shit outta your mind. Unless you're angry. Use the anger, but everything else is just a distraction."

I pour shampoo into my palm. "Says the perpetual bachelor."

"Yeah, how come you never had a family?" Cory asks Kane.

I give Cory credit, he's got balls. He's always asking questions as if Kane is The Godfather of hockey.

"First of all, I still have time for a family, and second, I never found someone who was worth it."

"Worth it?" Cory asks.

"Worth me not experiencing the once-in-a-lifetime opportunity of being a professional hockey player that not everyone gets. Don't get me wrong, I was never interested in the puck bunny delight, but I like being able to give my all to my career. Until I find a woman worth the distraction, that's how it's gonna be. Maybe once I hang up my skates, I'll start looking."

Cory shrugs. "Makes sense, I guess."

"I know you're all hung up on that girl from Ford's wedding, and that's why you've spent so much time giving the bunnies attention, but you need to forget her. You're in your prime. Once"—Kane looks over at Aiden, then lowers his voice—"you get more time out there, you're gonna need to put that shit out of your head before it ruins your game. Don't go into this pining over some girl like you're in high school." He glances in my direction.

I shake my head but don't respond. No one understands Imogen and me.

Cory nods as though he's thinking about it, so I make a mental note to pull him aside at some point and tell him not to take Kane's advice. He just needs to be true to himself.

As I shut off the shower to head back to the changing area, I hear a woman yelling. A group of the guys are all peering around the corner of the hallway that leads into the locker room like high school students might if the teacher's boyfriend showed up during class.

I can hear now that it's Imogen. "You need to trust people. Lena married you and she's raising Annabelle as her own. She can take care of her. And as for me, I'm fine. I can handle myself when it comes to Warner."

A few guys turn around and look at me.

Ford says something, but I struggle to hear him with the showers at my back.

"He did it to me. Not you, Ford. Me. So it's my call what happens."

Ford says something else, and luckily, Tweetie asks what Ford said because he couldn't hear either.

"He asked her if something is going on between her and Langley," Train says, eyeing me, as do five other guys.

Shit. I want Imogen to admit it, but I'm not sure this is the best moment.

"No! Do you think I'm crazy?" she says.

Coach comes out of his office, and everyone tries to act as if nothing was happening.

"What the hell is going on in here? Imogen Jacobs, get out of my locker room!" Coach holler.

Damn, I can't say it doesn't hurt that she didn't admit we're seeing one another, but I think I've heard her deny she's dating me more than the opposite over the course of our lives. Hopefully, one day soon, that changes.

CHAPTER 22

"Take me home."
-Imogen

Imogen

I buy my ticket to the movie and purposely show up while the previews are on, so the theater is dark and no one will see us together.

I hate that we can't even go see a new movie together, but it's what's best for now. Instead, we're at one of the cinemas that shows old movies. When I was growing up, it used to be black-and-white films, but now they show the movies I grew up with. It makes me feel old.

It's a nineties night, so *Clueless* and *There's Something About Mary* are on the bill. It's not very busy, so it isn't hard to spot Warner when I step into the darkness.

Sitting down next to him, I immediately thank him for getting popcorn and my favorite movie candy, Twizzlers.

"You're a lifesaver," I say, digging my hand into his popcorn. "I'm starving. Didn't have time to eat lunch because I had to set up your interviews for tomorrow. Then I had to go over rules. You know how many women asked to kiss you on the cheek?" I eat what I have in my hand and go in for more. "I said a hug was fine. But if they get handsy, I'm going to intervene."

He doesn't say anything, and the movie starts. I don't remember him as a rule follower and I know you're not supposed to talk in the theater, but I thought that whole handsy comment would have earned me some sort of joke in return.

"Are you going to share those Twizzlers?" I ask.

"Imogen," Warner whispers, not from beside me.

I stiffen and look to my left.

"Other way."

I jolt in my seat when I look left again and see that I'm not sitting beside Warner. "Oh no."

"Oh yes," Warner says, standing at the end of the aisle and smiling ear to ear. "Please excuse us, and the popcorn's on us." He hands the guy a twenty.

"I'm so sorry," I say. It's all I can do to slide out of the row without blocking the view of anyone else.

"It's okay. I thought it was my lucky night," he says, and I'm glad he can see the humor in the situation.

"You're never living that down," Warner whispers, escorting me to our row. Once we're seated, he hands me a tub of popcorn. "*Our* popcorn." Then he hands me Twizzlers. "Your licorice."

"Thank you." My face is still hot with embarrassment.

"I'm a little offended you can't recognize me."

I look around where we're seated, which is behind the guy I sat next to. "Warner?"

"Yeah?"

"You saw me go by you."

He nods and looks as if he's trying to hold back a smile. "I did."

"And you just let me sit next to that man and take his popcorn?"

He swings his arm around my shoulders. "I had my eye on you the entire time."

I snuggle into his side and throw a handful of popcorn at him. "Watch your back, Langley."

"Ohhh... I'm shaking." I swat his stomach and he holds me tighter, kissing my cheek. "I missed you like crazy."

And then all is forgiven because I missed him too. Last night I demanded I sleep at my place because I wanted to prove to myself I could. I second-guessed my decision the minute he left, and I was alone.

We watch the first movie, but because we're both too eager to spend time doing something we can't do together in public, we decide to skip the second screening. It was a nice thought and a great way for us to be in public together without anyone knowing, but I want to be alone with him.

"I'll go first," he whispers. "But don't take that as an invitation to spend more time with your other boyfriend." He chuckles and squeezes my hand before standing and leaving the movie theater.

I wait for three or four minutes. There's no reason we can't just run into each other, right? We could be talking about the interview I have set up for him.

The minute I walk out of the small theater, I see a small swarm of women around a very smiley Warner. I stand back and watch him sign autographs, pose for pictures, and entertain them with jokes. So far, I'd say I've been successful in making him more recognizable by the public. Jana told me attendance and sales of his jerseys are up too. In listening to the women, my theory is proven correct. These women didn't know who he was until recently.

A blonde approaches him. She's very touchy. "My husband took me to a game the other night. You guys spend a lot of time in the sin bin. That's what you call it, right?"

Warner looks around and spots me but doesn't linger long enough for the women to follow the direction of his gaze. "Yeah, Los Angeles can play dirty."

"And you have to play dirty right back," a brunette says with a baby voice.

I inwardly roll my eyes.

"My husband says you're the best player on the team now. You and Aiden Drake," another woman chimes in. "Ford Jacobs has lost his edge this season. Do you think it's because he got married?"

Warner laughs. "No."

"The baby?" the same woman asks.

"No." Warner seeks me out again and smiles.

This time he does grab the attention of the women and their heads turn in my direction.

"Oh, are you on a date?" the blonde asks, moving my way.

The brunette has her phone in hand, and I see her preparing to take a picture.

"She's just my friend," Warner is quick to say.

"Do I know you? I feel like I do," the blonde says and stares at me.

"Great meeting you, ladies, have a nice girls' night out." Warner takes my hand and tugs me away from the wall.

Just before we turn a corner, we hear the woman say, "I know who she is! That's Ford Jacobs's sister."

Warner and I look at one another and bust out into a run down the street.

"Only you would find a group of women who could recognize me."

He leads us down another street and pulls out his key fob, unlocking the doors. "Get in the car."

He opens up the passenger door and I climb in, thankful for tinted windows and the fact that I Ubered here. I feel like those women might have followed me to my car and cornered me otherwise.

He slides into the driver's seat a second later. "One day, every woman who approaches me will know that I'm yours."

My heart melts. Mostly because I know he means that. A small part of me can't wait for that to happen, and the more time we spend together, the more impatient I'm becoming for it.

"Coming home with me?"

I look out the window. If we go home, we'll have sex, which is amazing, but I want more. I love being at home with him, but I want us to be able to do things too. It's more evident than ever that the decision to keep this from Ford is what's causing this difficulty.

"Walk on the beach? It's getting dark."

"Anything you want." He straightens in his seat and buckles up, starting his SUV.

THE BEACH HAS a slight chill since the winter months are fast approaching. We're walking hand in hand with the moon hanging above the water.

"How's Morgan?" he asks.

"She's good. At college. Probably will make my parents the proudest of the three of us." I laugh.

"Your dad finally came around with Ford, huh? Remember those dinners our senior year? I was scared shitless of your dad. Especially since I was the one doing what Ford wanted to."

I nod, hating those times. I hate that Warner had to see my family like that. "They just kind of reconciled recently. Annabelle helped a lot."

"I imagine she would. She's a beautiful baby, but I mean, you Jacobs aren't lacking in the genetics department."

"Are you complimenting my brother?" I hit him with my shoulder, and he pretends that he's going to go in the water but recovers at the last minute.

"I only have eyes for one Jacobs and we both know who that is."

"Bennie?"

We both laugh at the mention of my parents' personal chef.

"Is he here? Did he come down with your parents?" I ask.

"He did. Said he's not much closer to Hawaii, but at least other people wear Hawaiian shirts here. They spend a lot of their time here now."

He shakes his head. "I like that guy. I think he always saw past my facade."

"Probably. I've never met a man who can gossip as well as a bunch of church ladies but keep so much inside. I know he knew about us long before we were open about our relationship."

"Do you ever wish we would have told people sooner?"

I shake my head. "No."

"Really?"

"I liked getting to know you in that theater room. We made memories there that made it hard to get over you even after things went bad."

He squeezes my hand. "I remember how excited I'd get knowing you were waiting for me. I'd pretend to sleep until Ford passed out. All I wanted to do was go to you."

I let go of his hand and wrap my hand around his waist. He puts his arm around my shoulders.

"Thanks," he whispers before kissing the top of my head.

"For what?"

"This. The second chance."

I squeeze him harder. "I'm not sure I could have carried on with my life had I not given us a try." It's hard to admit that to him, to be this vulnerable, but it's true. At least now I'll know. However things work out, I won't have to wonder.

He stops us and holds me against him. "Do you think we're soul mates?"

I chuckle and slap his chest, but his face is serious. "I don't know, but why would I meet my soul mate just so he can leave me for years?"

He shrugs. "Maybe we had to grow up. Maybe we had to lose it to appreciate what we had. Maybe we had to be independent for a while."

The talk of how long we've been separated takes my mind to places I wish it didn't. "Can I ask you a question? I told myself I don't care, but I think I need to know."

He stares at me for a long moment, then his hand glides along my cheek. "You want to know about other women?"

I nod. "I'm sorry. I hate that I have to ask, but I mean, Ford had a reputation. You didn't, that I know of, but..."

"Hey, normal couples give numbers all the time, right? That said, I don't want yours. I don't even want to think about you being with anyone else." His jaw flexes.

I nod and look at his chest.

He puts his finger under my chin and brings it up so our eyes meet. "Not as many as you think. I can't say none, but I meant what I said. My heart has always been yours. That never changed, so the women I did have, it was just sex. Nothing more."

"You never tried to move on?" I hold my breath, waiting for his response.

He sighs. "Once. I thought maybe I could do it, but the

comparison game started, and she never measured up to you. That wasn't fair to her, so I ended things."

"I'm scared," I admit.

"Me too." He pulls me into his chest and rests his chin on my head. "Me too."

And I feel it within him. The tension I know won't be resolved until Ford knows about us. Meaning, if I ever want to feel like this relationship is real, I have to tell Ford, no matter what his reaction is.

"Take me home," I whisper into Warner's chest.

"Always," he says and turns us around to head back to his place.

I asked him to take me home, but the truth is, I feel like I'm home whenever I'm with him.

CHAPTER 23

Warner

"I don't want to go," I whine to Imogen, who's getting ready for the interview event I have to do today. At least she's dressing down. Makes it feel less like work, even if it is.

She's decked out in jeans and a Florida Fury sweatshirt.

"I think you should wear my jersey in honor of me having to do an exhausting number of interviews." I lie on my bed and stare at the ceiling.

She crawls over me, still putting in one earring. "You do, huh? You don't think people will suspect anything?"

I sit up and wrap my arms around her waist, keeping her in place. "It's possible. Go check the top drawer."

When I release her, she finishes clasping her earring and walks over to my dresser, which by now is already half her dresser. I took the bottom two drawers and fit everything else in the shelves of my closet.

"How come I feel like I don't have a choice?" She holds my jersey up to her body.

"You do, but I'm gonna be really disappointed if you don't wear it." I pretend to pout, and she strips off her sweatshirt and puts on the jersey. "Now lose the pants and it's perfect."

Her fingers go to the button of her jeans. I watch as she

pulls them down her legs. So. Fucking. Hot. Nothing prepares you to see the woman you love wear your jersey with hardly any clothes underneath.

"Come here," I say, spreading my legs.

"We don't have much time."

"We have enough. And I can be a little late." My fingers delve under her silk panties, grabbing her ass in both hands. "God, will there ever be a time I don't want you?"

Her fingers thread through my hair and she steps into me, putting my eyes at breast level. "I hope not."

"You don't have to hope, it's never gonna happen."

She hugs me. I have to say, her hugs are the best. She says so much in her touch.

"How about I relax you before we head out? I know you hate these things," she whispers, her hand sliding between our bodies and palming my hard dick.

"No objections there." I lean back on my arms, and she kisses me on the lips, sliding her tongue into my mouth before descending down my body.

I help her pull down my track pants since I've yet to get ready. My dick springs out as soon as she pulls down the elastic waist to rest under my balls.

"This image is going to be burned into my brain," I say, watching her grasp the base of my dick and direct the tip to her luscious lips. She slides her tongue out and twirls it around the tip, and it takes all my control not to lift my ass up and push past her plump lips. "Fuck, Gen."

She continues to use her mouth on my cock while locking her gaze with mine. It's all I can do not to come when she takes me as far back in her throat as she can, then slides back up, her tongue taking over while her fist jerks me off.

"Come here," I say, attempting to get her up, but she shakes her head.

"I'm the boss this time."

Chuckling, I put both hands out to my sides. "You will be fucking me with that jersey on later though."

"Deal."

She goes back to giving me the best blow job of my life. There's something special about watching the woman you love worship your cock. I can barely think of anything else except the pleasure I'm receiving right now.

It isn't long until I'm thrusting into her fist, my orgasm inevitable. "I'm gonna come."

But she stays in place. Fuck, I couldn't love this woman more.

I grip the sides of the mattress and come in her mouth. She swallows it down, then licks me clean.

"Now you better come here." I lift my arms in front of me.

She raises off the bed and I kiss the ever-loving shit out of her.

"We really need to get going," she says, removing herself from my arms. "And you need to shower."

I groan and roll off the bed. My phone rings and I check the screen and see that it's my mom. I've been dodging her calls recently because she has a big mouth. That, and I can't lie to her. Until Imogen and I come out, I have to be careful.

"Who's that?" Imogen asks.

"My mom."

"How is she?"

"I don't know because I haven't talked to her recently. I can't lie to her about us, so I'm putting it off until we tell everyone." I step into the shower. "Besides, she probably already knows something is up and has her friend Udessa doing her tarot cards."

"Does it upset you that you can't tell her?" she asks.

I can tell from her tone it upsets her that we can't talk openly about our relationship, but what choice do we have? At some point, we have to come out. I thought dating in secret would be fun and forbidden like it was back in high school. We'd get to know one another, get to the place we were at before, then tell everyone. But I'm starting to have second thoughts, because we can't be a real couple when we're in hiding.

"I mean, I want everyone to know we're together, but it'll happen eventually." I peek my head out of the shower. "Right?"

She smiles and pushes my head back in. "Yes."

***

WE ARRIVE OUTSIDE THE ARENA, where there's a setup for this interview thing. There's a couch on a platform, and behind the couch is a giant picture of yours truly, either from a warm-up or a practice because my helmet is off.

"Where did you get that?" I ask Imogen.

She laughs. "I took it."

"You did?"

"Pretty impressive, right? It's easy when the subject looks like you."

"Tell me, Miss Jacobs, have you used that picture late at night when you dig into your drawer?"

"Why, Mr. Langley, a lady never tells."

I can't stop laughing. I reach out before I think better of it, then I clutch my hand into a fist and push it into the pocket of my jeans. "I'll get it out of you later."

"You think tickling is a truth serum," she whispers while we pretend she's giving me instructions.

"With you, it is."

We stare at one another, and if we were anywhere else, we'd be kissing right now.

"Look who it is, our golden boy!" Drake shouts from the other side of the fence. He's holding an iced coffee and Saige is next to him, shaking her head.

"Our boy's growing up so fast." Tweetie pretends to wipe tears from his eyes.

Tweetie seemed a little perturbed at the beginning of the season that I'd been slotted in on the starting lineup, but we'd had a conversation about it last week and put any animosity to rest. We both agree that what's best for the team is what's most important. Still, he made it clear he's going to be working to get back on the starting lineup. Let him. I enjoy the competition.

I fully turn around and I can't believe that Drake, Maksim, Tweetie, and Cory are all there.

"Kane sends his regards. He doesn't do this bullshit anymore," Cory says, raising his hands. "His words, not mine."

"Imogen, how do we get a spot on the roster? I have some questions to ask." Tweetie raises his hand.

"Sorry, all spots are filled." She gives him a saccharine smile.

We walk over to the group, and I shake hands with everyone.

"Good thing Ford declined," Tweetie's girlfriend, Tedi, says, eyeing my jersey on Imogen.

"Oh, you know, since we're promoting him, it just made sense." Imogen shrugs as though it's nothing.

"Yeah, I mean, I hate wearing Tweetie's number."

"Say it again, woman." He picks her up firefighter style and twirls her around. She can't stop laughing and I see how they're the perfect fit.

"After you finish this, we're headed to Flappy's. Wanna join?" Maksim asks.

Flappy's is a bar and restaurant, but they have shuffleboards, darts, and pool tables.

"Want a rematch?" I ask Imogen, referring to when we were at Ford's island resort wedding and played.

She narrows her eyes. "Sure, we're in. Will Ford be there?"

I feel as though we both hold our breath.

"No." Drake doesn't have to say anything else.

As great as it feels to have my teammates here to support me, it sucks that Ford's not one of them.

"I better go get ready. Thanks for coming, guys."

"We don't pass up a chance to make fun of each other. We have a few bets on how many kisses and hugs you'll get. I better win." Drake points at me.

"I'll do my best."

Imogen follows me to the makeup trailer. It's really just to get me away from everyone.

"You really like that, huh?"

I look over from the chair. "What?"

"That they came to support you. That they feel like you're part of this team."

I nod, then shrug. "I love the feeling of being on a team. You know after everyone found out I was the poor kid, I lost that at Lauder. For the first few years in the league, I shied away from making any friends in the organization, telling myself that if I got traded, I didn't want to leave close friends behind. But when I was with the Sharks, I found a group of guys I gelled with, and we did a lot together. It's like having a second family. The only problem is I don't want to steal Ford's." I frown.

She sits on my lap and wraps her arms around my neck. "If he'd get his head out of his ass, it wouldn't be a problem."

I take the opportunity to kiss her, and as I slide my tongue into her mouth and feel her relax in my arms, the trailer door opens. I push her off me and she flies halfway across the small room.

"I don't care if you two are fucking." The woman comes in and places her makeup bag on the table. "I'm serious. I don't know who you are except that you play hockey. I don't follow it and I have no interest in it. Even if I did, I'd keep my mouth shut. That's how you stay employed in this business."

Imogen and I share a look.

"Seriously, I can go if you two wanna get it on before I pretty this boy up." She waits for a second with her hand on her hip.

"We're good," Imogen says, shaking her head, dodging all eye contact.

I chuckle, and the woman gets to work while Imogen goes back outside to make sure everything is set up to her liking. Once my makeup is on—which is minimal at my insistence, since this is more a live social media thing and not like being on television—I leave the trailer and see that the crowd has quadrupled.

"What the hell?"

"Isn't it great? I love this." Imogen claps.

I try to feed off of Imogen's excitement, but this isn't me. I hate everything about this. I want to turn around and go back into the trailer. But then I look at Imogen again and see the sparkle in her eyes. For a moment, I wonder how our life together will be. I shy away from crowds and people, and she steps into them. I shake away that feeling because I know we might be different, but I'm confident we'll find a balance.

"Okay, sit." She points toward the couch.

"Should I bark too?"

She laughs and absentmindedly touches my thigh. She's quick to realize her mistake and retracts her hand so fast no one probably noticed. Still, I can't help but feel as though we're on borrowed time when it comes to sneaking around.

"Is there a Hillary *W*? Come on down!" Imogen calls out as though she's the announcer for *The Price is Right*.

"Hey, Bob Barker, can you make sure no one tries to overstay their welcome?"

She sighs and gives me her look. The one to suggest I'm being grumpy.

Hillary is a thirty-something woman with dyed blond hair based on her dark eyebrows. She's dressed in head-to-toe Florida Fury gear and has my number painted on her cheeks.

"Love the number," Imogen says. "Have a seat, Hillary."

I wasn't aware Imogen would be the host.

The woman does, and I put my hand out between us. "Nice to meet you, Hillary. I'm Warner."

Hillary blushes. "Nice to meet you, and I know who you are."

"Okay, Hillary, you have three minutes and forty seconds to ask Mr. Langley any question you like, and he has to answer honestly." Imogen sets the timer and steps off the stage, leaving me with Hillary.

"Okay, well, you're single, so I was wondering what your type is?" Hillary asks.

I lean back in my chair. "Well, she has to have a sense of humor. Personality is huge for me. Intelligent, have ambition and goals. Compassion for others, good morals." I'm basically describing Imogen. "Anyone who can have a good time doing nothing is the woman for me."

"High standards, Langley!" one of the guys shouts through the crowd.

"Hey, no questions from the crowd, please," Imogen says. "Anything else, Hillary?"

She looks as though she wants to shrink into a ball. "Can I have a hug?"

"Sure." I stand and hug her, then she's quick to leave the stage.

I go through more people, two guys who actually ask about hockey stuff and three women who ask about my childhood and charity work. Every time someone asks me for a hug, Drake lifts his hands in the air, keeping count.

Then a little girl who can't be older than ten joins me.

"This is Rena Torres, and she has a question for you." Imogen nods at her to go ahead.

"Shoot." I give Rena a smile.

"Do you think there's a place for girls in hockey? I have four brothers and I'm the only girl. The baby. They never let me play."

"Well, Rena, that's my easiest question of the day. There is absolutely a place for girls in hockey. The world might be a little slow in acknowledging the female hockey players out there, but change is coming, and you just make sure you practice so you're ready. And challenge your brothers. Show them you can hang with them. If they keep saying no, give us a call. The Florida Fury will happily slap the puck around with you."

Her eyes flare wide enough to fall out of their sockets if they weren't attached. "Really?"

"Heck yeah!" my teammates yell over the crowd.

"Hear that? Drake is already shaking in his skates."

Her smile grows wider. "Can I ask one more question?" She holds up her pointer finger.

"Of course, sweetie," Imogen answers for me.

"Well, I don't want to take up extra time." She looks at her, unsure.

"That's okay, Bob Barker runs this show, and he says it's fine," I say.

Imogen and I laugh because Rena looks confused.

"Are you lonely? My mom said you live by yourself, and you just moved here. We used to move around a lot and sometimes I'd be lonely."

"Ah, well, everyone gets lonely sometimes, but lately... I've been exploring this new city. Putting myself out there and getting to know people." I resist the urge to glance at Imogen and instead look in the direction of my teammates.

The little girl nods. "But my mom says everything is always better when she's with my dad and us. Wouldn't it be better if you had a family?"

I lean forward.

"I'm sorry, Rena—" Imogen starts, but I put up my hand.

"It's okay. Are you asking if I want a family, Rena?"

"Well, yeah." She shrugs. "My mom said sometimes guys like to stay single though." Her forehead wrinkles as though she doesn't quite understand that, and I chuckle.

I glance toward the front of the crowd and see her mother mouthing she's sorry. I smile to let her know it's okay.

"Actually, I very much want to have a family."

She squirms in her seat. "I told you, Mom!" Rena shouts, then scoots closer to me. "Do you have a girlfriend? I won't tell anyone." She puts her hand by her ear and the entire place laughs.

I lean in. "Are you sure you can keep a secret?"

She nods enthusiastically.

I cover up my mouth at her ear. "I do."

Her eyes widen, giving away my answer, and the whole crowd oohs and ahhs.

After Rena leaves the stage with a hug and kiss on the cheek, Imogen leans in close. "Jana's gonna kick your ass."

I lean in close to her, catching a whiff of her shampoo. "I told you a long time ago, I don't pretend to be someone I'm not anymore."

She stares at me for a long beat, then turns back to the crowd, announcing the next person.

CHAPTER 24

Imogen

"Don't stop," I pant as Warner takes control of my hips. We're on a small yacht he rented, and we've been down below more than up top. It started the minute I took off my cover-up. He pounced on me like a lion.

"I don't plan on it." He's sitting on the edge of the bed, and I'm on his lap with my back to his chest, reverse cowgirl style, my hands on his strong muscular thighs. He has all the control, and I'm more than happy to give it to him. "You're soaked. I might as well tell them to serve our candlelight dinner down here tonight. I'll just eat it off of you."

"Best. Idea. Ever." I gasp and moan as he drives in deeper and deeper with every thrust.

"Fuck, I hate this thing. Hold on." He pulls me off of him and I turn to find him fussing with a broken condom. "Let me get a new one."

"Wait." I take the condom from him.

"What?"

I pause, considering whether I'm really ready to say what's about to come out of my mouth and find that I am. "I'm on the pill. We don't need condoms. I mean, as long as you're clean."

"Of course, I wouldn't hide that from you. I'd never put

you at risk like that, Gen." He runs his knuckles down my cheek.

There have been times these past few weeks that I've reprimanded myself for not just spitting out the news to Ford and dealing with the repercussions. I'm a grown adult, after all, and he's being immature. Plus, he's not my father. But he was also the one who was there for me when Warner wasn't. Ford saw my pain and heartbreak more than anyone. Even Cici. I think it's because we both lost our number one person.

"I am too. Then... okay. Let's do this."

"Are you sure?" He looks at me, clearly unsure.

I nod, not wanting to make a big deal of it and bring us back to the past. When I got pregnant, we didn't use protection one time, but I was on the tail end of my period and thought I couldn't get pregnant during that time in my cycle. Turns out you don't know everything at seventeen.

I nod. "I am."

"Gen..."

I've clearly ruined the moment between us by bringing this up, but I want to feel him bare with nothing between us. I want us to have that connection.

"I want this. I do." I push him down on the bed and climb on top of him. There's still a hesitation in his actions, so I take his hands and place them on my breasts.

"I love you. You trust that, right?" He's so serious. I want to bring us back to that place we were minutes ago.

I nod.

"I'd never do what I did before."

"I know."

I rise on my knees, reach for his dick, and drag the head through my wetness, then I sink down on him. We both moan. He slowly circles his hips from beneath me, with little thrusts inside me.

"I'm ready to move at any pace you want me to." He brings his hand up my back and into my hair at the base of my skull.

"This is good," I say, enjoying the small kisses he's placing on my neck, as though he's cherishing me.

"I meant us. Telling Ford."

Seriously, he's picking now to discuss this? I know he's growing antsy, I am too, but we're in the middle of having sex.

"Okay, I'll think about it. Just don't stop."

His hands wander up and down my body as though he hasn't felt me hundreds of times before. "You're my future," he whispers.

I close my eyes, trying to concentrate on the sweet things he's saying. Words I've waited for so long to hear him say.

He rocks me up and down on his dick. My orgasm is slow to build, but the more he stays at the same pace, the more my body thrums with pleasure.

"You're mine," I say, and that declaration seems to unleash something inside him.

He rolls me onto my back and runs his hands up my arms, then links our fingers together. Grinding inside me, he stares into my eyes with an intensity that says I'm his. And I am. There's no question about that.

I wrap my legs around his waist, so my pelvic bone gets the satisfaction of the friction between us.

"I love you so fucking much, Gen." He buries his head in my neck, kissing my sweat-soaked skin, licking, sucking.

I tighten my arms around his shoulders, wanting to get as close as I can to him. He increases his pace, and our lips land on one another's in a frenzied kiss, mouths colliding, and before long, I know I'm going to come.

"Oh, Warner. Oh, God. Oh, I can't hold back."

"Don't."

My body tenses in his hold until I shudder from the intensity of my orgasm. He never lets me go and inhales a deep breath in my ear, releasing it a second later when he stills inside me, and I feel his cock pulse with his release. Still, he doesn't let me go.

We lie in the bed for another five minutes as if we both know everything is about to change and our time in secrecy is over. We have to come out if we want our relationship to survive. We just have to figure out when and how.

I'M up on the sundeck of the yacht, enjoying the especially nice day for this time of year, looking over the railing while Warner talks to the chef about tonight's meal. We dropped anchor about an hour ago and have just been enjoying each other's company.

This is the sweetest thing anyone has ever done for me. But I sense he did it for two reasons. The first is that it gets us away from prying eyes. The second because the money thing is really important to him, and this is his way of giving me the life he thinks I want. He's yet to get it through his thick skull that all I want in my life is him.

"IMOGEN! Is that you?"

I look to my right to find a speedboat beside us and Saige waving frantically. She and Aiden are there, along with Tweetie and Tedi.

"Where'd you get that beauty?" Tweetie asks. "Richie up there with you?"

I look behind me. No sign of Warner. "Um. No."

"You're on a date!" Tedi points. "Who's the guy? Does Ford know? Can I be the one to tell him? Pretty please?" She puts her hands in a prayer pose.

"Um."

"What's going on?" Saige asks, sensing my hesitation.

"Let's dock this shit boat and join Imogen and whoever her rich friend is," Tweetie says to Aiden.

"This is not a shit boat. It's brand new, and you were pretty impressed before we rolled up to a mini yacht."

"Exactly." Tweetie holds out his hands. "A mini yacht and this thing, there's no comparison."

"Sorry, no one can come up," I call to them.

"Because it's a date?" Tedi asks with a Cheshire cat smirk. "Oh, it's not Mr. Gerhardt's boat, is it?"

"He's married," I say with obvious disgust, because Mr. Gerhardt is nice and all but he could be my father—or my grandfather.

"Who else could it be? You haven't been on those sugar daddy sites, have you?" Saige laughs.

"It's really no one. But I should probably get back to him."

"Gen, I almost forgot." Warner steps out onto the deck.

"Who's that?" Tweetie asks.

They're too low to see who I'm talking to, so I openly shoo him away and shake my head.

"She's purposely not letting us meet him," Tweetie says.

"She's probably ashamed that you're ready to climb up their emergency ladder," Aiden tells him.

Warner's face freezes like if he only moves his eyes, they'll think he's a statue.

"Well, it was great seeing you guys, but I was just told we have to go. I'll, um, message you later, ladies." I walk away from the railing, then circle back. "Could you not mention this to Ford?"

"Stay away from the sugar daddies!" Tweetie points as though he's giving me a warning.

"Will do." I wave one more time and step back to Warner. We have to hide him. I shake my head. "Seriously, are they following us?"

"Drake?" Warner asks.

"How'd you know?" My brow furrows.

"I just remembered he said he's always out on his boat when we're not playing."

"And you forgot when you booked this?" I motion to the yacht surrounding us.

"I forgot, okay?" He seems affronted, then looks at the captain. "I'm gonna have to ask you to dodge that speedboat."

"Shouldn't be a problem." He raises the anchor, then pushes the boat into a high gear.

"Are you sure you forgot? Or did you purposely plan this, hoping it might happen?"

Warner points at himself. "Why would I try and plan that?"

"So we'd be caught! You clearly want us out in public."

"Yes! Yes, I do!" he yells. "I'm tired of being a secret. Sometimes I wonder if you just don't want to acknowledge us publicly so that you can bail if you decide to. It'd be a lot easier for you that way."

"Sir, your friends seem to want to race," the captain says.

We look back and sure enough, Aiden and Tweetie are laughing hysterically as they try to catch up to us.

I push Warner down to the deck. "They can't see you."

The captain looks at us funny.

"This is ridiculous. I thought I could do this. I actually

thought it would be fun like it was in high school, but it's not. It's not fun, it feels like you have one foot out the door. When I want to spend every waking moment with you. When I want to treat you like a fucking princess but get stopped at every turn."

I cock my head. "Princess? That's the word you choose?"

He stands. "Yes, is that a problem?"

"I think it's telling is all. You call me a princess and you rent this for a day. I don't need all this."

"Okay."

"I'm serious, Warner. I'm not some princess who needs the best of everything and will throw a fit when she doesn't get it."

He puts his hands on his hips, and it's really hard to concentrate with his abs on display like that. "I never said you were."

"Then why would you rent this?" I open my arms and twirl in a circle. "This isn't you."

The captain glances over his shoulder again. "I'm going to have to call the Coast Guard. Your friends are being irresponsible. They're going to get someone in an accident."

I grab Warner and drag him down the stairs to the deck, then head to the back of the boat.

"Stop this, Aiden!" Saige is yelling.

"I've got it under control," he yells back.

"You want to know who it is?" I shout at them.

"Don't do this on my account," Warner says, and I roll my eyes.

I pull him out of the darkness. "Warner Langley!"

I pull him toward me and plaster my lips to his. There's no sound from the boat behind us. Even their engine cuts off. We pull away while they're slowing in the water. All of their faces are in shock except for Aiden, who is pointing.

I just make out Aiden saying, "I fucking knew it!"

"Point proven, right Imogen?" Warner leaves me at the back of the boat and goes to the room below.

"Where are you going? I just outed us. I thought you'd be happy. Want to announce it on the Jumbotron the next game?"

He whips around and points at me. "I didn't want to push you into it. I wanted you to want to tell the world we're together. Have you ever wondered whether you truly love me or just the idea of me?"

"What?" I whisper and step back.

He starts packing his bag.

"What are you suggesting?" I ask, hurt by his accusation.

"I was your brother's best friend when you fell in love with me. I was the king of the school and now I'm Florida Fury's 'it' man. Are you sure you love *who* I am and not *what* I am?"

"If that was the case, why would I want to keep it a secret?" My voice is getting louder.

"Because it's something cute."

"I'm not thirteen, Warner."

"Exactly. You're twenty-seven and you can't face your brother to tell him you're in love with his enemy. How much will you sacrifice to make someone else happy?" He swings his bag over his shoulder. "I paid for the night, so enjoy yourself."

"You're really leaving?" I yell.

He turns to face me when he reaches the door. "I need some space. I think we both need to think about what we want, what we need from this relationship. I can't live in secret, but I love you, Gen. And I don't want to feel like I love someone more than they love me."

I shake my head. "You're being crazy."

"Am I? Who's more important in your life, Imogen? Ford or me?"

I open my mouth and shut it. My shoulders slump. "But…"

"Just think about it. If you think telling Ford would really do irreparable damage to your relationship, no explanation needed. He's your blood. You guys are tight, I get it."

Then he walks up the stairs and leaves me behind. It feels a lot like it did a decade ago, except this time, I feel as though I'm the one at fault.

CHAPTER 25

"Doctor Marc."

Warner

"Turn around and leave," I mumble to myself, but Aiden's front door opens before I can escape.

Saige stands in the doorway, barefoot and wearing a sundress. "Hey, Warner. Welcome."

"This is for you." I hand Saige a bottle of white wine.

She smiles when she sees the label. "How did you know?"

"Drake told me your favorite."

She laughs and waves me into the house. "He's the sweetest."

"Just the sweetest." I chuckle. I shrug off the light coat I'm wearing, and she waits to take it from me.

"Warner, I wanted to apologize for the other day on the water. Tweetie brings out the worst in Aiden and they thought they were having fun. I don't think any of us really thought it would be you. I mean, we thought you guys hated one another."

I put my hand up for her to stop rambling. "It's fine."

"And I promise none of us will say anything. We took an oath that day in the boat not to be the bearer of bad news." Saige is very animated when she talks. Her hands are in the air, her eyes show every emotion she's feeling.

"No worries. Speaking of... is Imogen here?"

"Not yet. I think she's coming with Ford and Lena. They were dropping Annabelle off at his parents." She leads the way down a hallway, then all I see is the Gulf out the back of the house. Drake's got a great place. "Warner's here," she announces to the room.

Tedi smiles. "Hey, Warner."

"Tedi." I nod in hello.

"How are you?" Paisley asks, then sips her wine.

"Good, thanks."

"The boys are outside," Saige says, as if I need a reprieve from talking to the women.

"Thanks."

I head outside, and sure enough, Drake, Maksim, Cory, Tweetie, and Kane all sit around a card table, playing.

"You're late," Cory calls me out.

All the attention comes to me, and I go around the table, shaking hands and saying hello.

I'm late because it took me this long to decide if I was really coming here tonight or not. Imogen and I haven't spoken since I left the boat last weekend, and talking for the first time here in front of everyone isn't exactly ideal. But we need to talk.

I fucked up. I know I did. My abandonment issues courtesy of my father coming out to play and getting the best of me. I just couldn't help but feel like she had one foot out the door because she wouldn't publicly acknowledge who I was to her—the same as my absentee father. I need to explain to her. I feel as though she's slipping through my fingers.

"Okay, beer's in the cooler over there. Wine's with the women. Hard stuff in that bar." Aiden points out where everything is.

"Thanks." I grab a beer and unscrew the lid, sitting on the edge of the stone wall and watching them play cards.

"You want to take my spot?" Maksim asks.

"Nah, I'm good."

We talk about the season and how shitty things are looking for us. Someone mentions that Ford still won't pass me the puck, but truth is, I've grown so used to it, it doesn't bother me anymore. Imogen hasn't been to a game this week, and she hasn't asked me to do any promotional shit.

"No more bringing up depressing crap at my party," Aiden says. "Babe, turn up the music," he calls loud enough to be heard inside.

"Babe!" she shouts. "This is a dinner party, not boys' night. Meaning the couples mingle together!"

"Well fuck, sorry, boys. Last hand." Aiden deals another hand, and everyone laughs.

After the guys finish playing poker, we head inside, where the dinner table is set for a shit ton of people. The doorbell rings as Saige and Aiden are talking about the fish —which does not bring the best out of them, I can tell you that.

"I'll get it," I offer so they can finish bickering.

"Perfect, thanks, Warner," Saige says and musters up a smile for me.

They go back to arguing in low voices.

"Oh, I was just about to get it," Cory says, meeting me by the door.

I swing open the door to find a guy dressed in scrubs with a bag over his shoulder. Who the hell is this?

"Hey, are you Shamrock?" he asks.

"No." I step back. "Let me get him."

"Oh, okay. You must be another guest then? I'm here for Imogen actually."

"Fuck," Cory whispers from behind me.

My head tilts and my hands fist at my sides. "Imogen

Jacobs?" I clarify, my heart plummeting to the depths of my stomach.

"Yeah. Is she here?" He sort of angles himself to the side to try to see past me.

"No."

"Oh wow. Okay. I thought I was going to be late. Hence the reason I didn't change out of my scrubs when I left work." He motions at the blue cotton. "Do you mind?"

"Oh." I slide out of his way.

"Who are you?" Aiden joins us and looks between me, Cory, and the guy.

"This is Shamrock," I say to the guy looking for Imogen. Asshole. Who doesn't change before a party, no matter how late they're going to be? Especially if you don't even know anyone at the party? Are we supposed to be impressed that he's a doctor?

"Good to meet you. I'm Marc. I'm here for Imogen, but..." He nods to me. "He said she's not here yet. Mind if I change really quick?"

Aiden shakes his head a bit as though he must have misheard him. I know the feeling. "Who are you here for?"

"He's here for Imogen," Cory fills in the blanks.

"I have the right house, correct? You all play for the Fury?" He looks between the three of us.

"Yeah, yeah. Okay, first door on your left is the guest bed and bath." Aiden motions to the stairs.

"Great, mind if I take a quick shower?"

I raise my eyebrows at Aiden, and he looks as though he has no idea how to respond except to nod. "Sure."

"Perfect." Marc walks up the stairs but comes back right away. "And if my date shows up, tell her I'll be down in a second." He gives us a wink.

"And by date you mean..." Aiden still seems confused.

"Imogen," he says like we're idiots.

"Right. Right." Aiden nods.

"Thanks." He gives us a fake pistol shoot with the hand that isn't holding his bag and heads up the stairs.

"What the hell is going on?" Cory asks as soon as Marc's out of earshot.

When we went out after practice last night, I told him and Kane everything. I have to start trusting people and they've been nothing but loyal to me. Getting it off my chest felt good, but at the same time... she brought a fucking date tonight?

My anger simmers right below the surface and I don't know how long I'll be able to contain it.

"I don't know." Aiden looks at me.

I roll my eyes. "Cory knows."

"Well then, what the fuck, man? Did you two break up?" Aiden yells but quiets his voice near the end of his sentence.

"We didn't really break up. We're taking a break. I'm giving her some space. Or at least I thought that's what we were doing."

Aiden runs his hand through his hair. "Haven't you ever seen *Friends*? You never take a break."

"I think I need the hard stuff." I leave them and head to the bar outside where Kane is talking with Tweetie, giving him advice on how to deal with being on the second line now.

Sometimes, you get lucky with a team and find real friends that feel like family. That's what it's starting to feel like here for me.

After pouring myself a vodka tonic with a lime, I sit down next to them.

"Who killed your puppy?" Tweetie asks me.

"Nothing. Beer just wasn't cutting it." I down the entire glass.

I didn't hear the doorbell, but I do hear the hellos from everyone and glance inside the house to see Ford and Lena. Imogen isn't with them, so I turn my attention back to the ocean.

"I was hoping Langley wouldn't show." Ford says to someone.

"Fuck off, Ford," Cory says and comes outside.

"Excuse me?" Sounds like Ford brought his attitude with him tonight. Perfect.

"Not tonight," Lena says. "It's one dinner. This is Aiden and Saige's party."

I turn around when I hear them come outside. "Kind of funny that Lena has to treat you like her second child."

"I do not have time for your bullshit tonight." Ford pours himself a scotch.

"Feeling's mutual." I kick off the wall, ready to thank Aiden and Saige and politely leave, when Imogen appears from the downstairs bathroom.

She stops when she sees me, and I stop at the patio door. I guess she thought I wouldn't come. I didn't want to, but these teammates are all I've got here. Then Marc walks down the stairs, smiles at Imogen, and walks right past her. What the hell am I missing?

I head inside, about to approach Saige, but Marc beats me to her. "Are you Imogen?"

What the hell is up with this guy?

"Um... no." She looks around. "She's right there. Imogen?" She points at the guy.

Marc turns around, and I step up to Saige to take my opportunity to leave. "Hey, Saige, where's Aiden? I think I'm going to just—"

She holds up her finger for me to wait a second.

"Hi, I'm Imogen."

I turn and see her smile politely at Marc, and it makes me want to punch him in the face.

"Oh, great. I'm Marc."

Imogen nods. "Nice to meet you. Why were you looking for me?"

"I'm your date." He holds his hands out at his sides like ta-da.

Saige and Paisley snicker next to me.

It's clear by Imogen's expression that she has no idea who Marc is. "Excuse me?"

"What a prick," I mumble.

Marc hears me and turns to narrow his eyes at me. "I'm sorry?"

"Not you. Her brother."

"Yeah, Ford told me to come. That it was a couples thing, and you needed a date." He turns back to Imogen.

"Where did he find you?" Tedi asks. I didn't even realize she was listening.

"I'm his podiatrist."

I chuckle and shake my head. "Well, good luck, you two. What a match." I smile brightly and walk away.

"FORD!" Imogen yells.

"AIDEN!" Saige shouts.

"TWEETIE! Oh, forget it. He'll just laugh. NEVER MIND!" Tedi yells.

"Let's go get a drink, Dr. Marc," Paisley says, escorting him outside.

I go to the living room along with everyone else, ready to see how this pans out.

Ford puts out his hand. "Marc, nice to see you could make it."

"Thanks. I got here a little bit ago. Showered and stuff."

Imogen looks at Saige. "He showered here?"

Aiden comes inside from out back. "I was under the assumption he was a doctor. Like an emergency room doctor or something. Not the guy who files away Ford's bunions." Aiden strides over to Saige as he says to Imogen, "So Ford brought you a date and you have no idea who he is?"

"Bingo," Imogen says with irritation.

"He's literally gone off the cliff." Aiden shakes his head.

"Well, set another place," Saige says.

"Actually." I raise my hand. "No need. I'm gonna head out."

"No, you're not." Aiden heads into their dining room and I follow. "We have to be stuck with crazy, so do you. We're a team and we're in this together."

"You can't chain me to the chair."

"Want to watch me?" He slides the chairs down the table, then comes to grab an extra chair from the kitchen. "Maybe I should sit Ford at a kid's table since he's acting like a child."

I blow out a breath, unsure what the hell to do at this point.

"You're not still thinking about asking for a trade, are you?" Aiden asks.

I shrug. I'd said that earlier this week when I was angry that Imogen hadn't reached out to me and Ford was on my back. I was angry at everything and I just wanted out of Florida, but I didn't really mean it. Ford's the one who can't play well with others. Why should I bow out?

"You're leaving?" Imogen outs herself as an eavesdropper and steps into the dining room.

Aiden takes that as his cue to leave. "I gotta go get silverware."

"No. I just... no, I'm not," I say. "Sorry to disappoint you."

"Warner," she says, tilting her head as though I'm the idiot.

"It's been a week, Gen."

She looks down. "I'm aware."

"Okay. I get it."

"Get what?"

"Get your answer. Ford approves of Dr. Marc, so that's good, huh?" I go to slide past her, but she puts her hand on my chest. I stare down at it.

"You were unfair that day," she says.

"I was. I know I was and for that, I apologize. Most of what I said was just churned up daddy issues I shouldn't have taken out on you. Still doesn't change the fact that after a week, you can't decide."

"I've been busy at work. I'm—"

"You're scared. The funny thing is, the old Imogen wasn't scared of anything, especially not her brother. I'm the one who was hesitant back in high school."

"That's not true. I was scared," she says.

"Of what?"

"You! I've always been scared of you and the ability you had to make me happy or sad. My worst nightmare came true ten years ago, so maybe understand that being completely vulnerable with you is hard for me."

I step forward, then step back. "You said you forgave me. I'm not sure what else I can do to get you to trust me."

"That's just it. I don't know either."

"Then Dr. Marc it is." I don't let her hold me back this time and I walk out of the room.

Imogen storms past me and heads outside to Ford. She

drags him by the shirtsleeve off Aiden's deck and onto the beach.

I grab my jacket off the hook near the front door, figuring I'll sneak out, but my keys aren't in my pockets.

"Where are my keys?" I say more to myself than anyone.

Tweetie joins me near the door. "Let's play a game of hot or cold. Right now, you're in the arctic."

I run my hand through my hair and clench the roots. Maybe being part of the crew isn't all it's cracked up to be.

CHAPTER 26

"I never asked you to choose."

Imogen

"What the hell are you thinking? You can't just fix me up with someone without my knowledge," I yell at Ford on the beach outside Aiden's house. I'm so embarrassed.

"I didn't want you to feel left out."

"I wouldn't. They're all my friends, and my colleagues, too. Plus, Cory, Kane, and Warner aren't with anyone."

"Don't even mention Warner to me."

"Why?" I want to throw myself on the sand and kick and scream like a toddler. I hope Annabelle is the worst of the worst toddlers. And preteen. And teenager.

"Because I'm sick of hearing his name! Even tonight, dropping off Annabelle, Mom asked about him. What does she care?"

That surprises me. I feel my forehead crease. "Why is she asking about him?"

"It doesn't matter." He goes to walk away, but I grab his sleeve and pull him back.

"Yes, it does."

"She wanted to know if anything was going on with you two. I told her absolutely not, that I forbid it."

My head snaps back. "You forbid it?"

"That's right. He's no good for you. Look what he did to you."

"Dinner!" Saige yells from the deck.

Ford moves to walk away from me, but I tug him back again. "And if I would have forbidden you from being with Lena?"

He guffaws. "Okay, Imogen."

"Are you saying you wouldn't listen to me?" I cross my arms.

"There's nothing wrong with Lena. Now Warner, where do I start?"

I huff, but he doesn't even notice how pissed off he's made me. "But Marc, he's the man for me, huh?"

He shrugs. "Could be."

I nod a few times. "Okay, let's see about that. Dinner's ready. Don't want to be late."

I stomp through the sand, up onto the deck, get the sand out of my heels, then head into the house. Warner watches me as I pass him.

"I guess I can stay for dinner. Wouldn't want to miss the show." He follows me to the dining room.

By the time the three of us enter, the only free spots are two chairs beside each other on one side of the table and an empty seat directly across from them.

Warner covers my hand with his on the back of the single seat. "I'll take that one, so you can sit next to Dr. Marc."

I slide my hand out. "That's sweet of you." I make sure my voice is syrupy sweet.

"I'm sweet like that. Remember?" He winks, and I cock my jaw to the side.

I round the table and Dr. Marc pulls out the chair for

me. I thank him once he's got me snug into the table. I'm right across from Warner. I guess I like to torture myself.

"We want to thank you all for coming tonight. You're some of our dearest friends and we value the time we get to spend with you all. And well, Dr. Marc." Saige smiles at the uninvited guest, shrugging at Aiden when his expression clearly asks why she's addressing him. "Please enjoy yourselves. Let's dig in."

"That was a beautiful speech," Marc says to Saige.

"Thank you. Warner, please pass the bread," she says. Her smile grows more fake the longer this carries on. "Someone told everyone to bring my favorite white wine, so I hope everyone likes it."

"Hey, they all asked me what to bring. I wanted it to be something for you," Aiden says, arms out to his sides.

"So thoughtful. Thank you." Saige hands me a bottle to pass down.

"That reminds me. I'll be right back." Marc leaves the table.

When the front door opens and closes, I focus all my attention on Ford beside me, wishing I could shoot lasers with my eyes. "This is ridiculous. Now I have to play nice with a complete stranger who thinks he's my date?"

Ford shrugs. "He's a nice guy, and if you two hit it off, he's got a lot of connections."

I roll my eyes. "Do I even want to know?"

Lena mouths she's sorry, but I've had it with my brother pushing his own agenda.

"I bet he has a lot of connections with lotions. Do you think all podiatrists have a foot fetish?" Cory asks.

Everyone at the table laughs but sobers up when the front door opens and shuts again. In walks Marc, but now he's wearing Crocs and has a big bag that he hands to Saige. "I was running late and couldn't stop to get you wine. But this is like a little gift for everyone to take home. Don't leave home without them." He raises his finger and laughs at his own joke.

Saige leans back in her chair and lifts a case of insoles from the bag. "That's very nice of you." She grabs a few more. "Look, babe, insoles for everyone."

"Throw one of those down here," Tweetie says, and she does. He catches it as though he's blocking a shot on the goal.

"Two points for you, Tweet," Marc says, holding two fingers in the air.

Everyone is polite enough not to correct him that you only score one point in hockey, unlike basketball.

"What a unique gift to bring. Isn't he sweet, Imogen?" Warner smiles wide at me. "What do you give away on Halloween, Dr. Marc?"

"Nail files. I'd do clippers, but I'd probably get complaints from the parents."

Warner pretends to laugh. "Yeah, I can see that. You don't wanna have to deal with that."

"Sure don't." Marc smiles, oblivious that Warner is mocking him.

I kick Warner under the table, and he looks around. "You don't have a dog, do you, Saige?"

"No, why?"

Warner eyes me. "No reason. Thought something ran up against my leg."

Lucky for me, no one catches on to his insinuation.

Midway through dinner, Marc leans in close to me. "I meant to tell you, you should consider more sensible shoes. High heels are no one's friends."

"Bite your tongue!" Maksim says.

"Agreed!" Warner raises his hand.

All I envision is how much Warner enjoys the tips of my heels digging into his ass when he fucks me. My face burns in a full flush.

"Are you hot, Imogen? You look hot," Warner says, surely knowing full well what I'm thinking.

"Sure, they're sexy," Marc goes on. "But is putting a loved one's health in jeopardy worth the risk of wearing them?"

"Sorry, Doc, I'm not giving up my heels," I say.

"Well, I have some great alternatives. Come to the office sometime and I can show you. You'd be amazed. My mom was like you, but once I got her off the heels, she hasn't had any of the problems she was having."

"Yeah, maybe. What made you want to be a podiatrist?" I ask.

"I love feet. They're what keeps us standing on the ground, you know? Heart doctors say you only have one heart. Well, you only have two feet. Unless you're a bad dancer, then you have two left feet." He chuckles.

Tedi groans.

"Very true. I'll have to remember that," I say politely.

"Yes, all you hockey players should come in. I've helped Ford a lot since he started to see me."

I turn in my seat. "Really? What's wrong with my brother's feet?"

"A doctor never gives out private information. Even to sisters." He smiles and I sigh, catching Warner's shit-eating grin. He seems to love that I'm in this position.

"That's good to know," I say.

"Maybe after dinner, we should all go out for a walk in the sand to get a natural pedicure," Warner suggests with an innocent expression.

"Great idea. Good exercise and good for your feet too.

Gets all those layers of dead skin off the bottoms of your feet."

"Can we please stop talking about feet? It's great that you have a kink for it, Doc, but it grosses me out," Kane says, digging into his meal.

"Sure thing. Who here goes to Merfest?" Dr. Marc looks around.

"Do you go?" Lena asks, leaning as far as she can over the table. "I'd never heard of it until I came here." She smacks Ford's arm. "Did you hear that? He goes to Merfest."

"I heard the guy," Ford says, sounding as though Marc's disappointed him by bringing it up. "So you like to dress up?"

"I do. You should join me, Imogen. You know, if we're still dating."

Marc laughs, but my eyes lock with Warner across the table and I swallow past the dryness coating my throat. I've missed him like crazy this past week. And now we're at a dinner party, at odds with each other when we should be here as a couple.

Warner was right. I am scared. Scared that if we make it official and tell my brother, Ford will be proven right at some point. I mean, I wholeheartedly believe Warner loves me and wouldn't repeat his mistakes from the past, and I do forgive him for those mistakes, but then why am I still punishing him for them?

And why is my brother still getting a free pass when what he did was just as bad?

"I was just kidding," Dr. Marc says. He waves his hand in front of my face because my gaze is still locked on Warner's.

Warner tilts his head, wondering what I'm doing.

Getting my head out of my ass, that's what.

"You're very beautiful. I'm sure you have a lot of guys beating down your door," Marc says to me.

"Just one."

"What?" Ford's head whips in my direction. "Who?"

"Um…" Tedi says. "Am I the only one seeing this?"

"I'm sorry," I say to Warner.

"Me too," he says in return.

I clear my throat. "I'm sorry, Marc, but I'm taken."

I stand from my seat and crawl over the table to Warner, avoiding the food, and plant a huge kiss on his lips.

"I think you could have walked around, but…" Saige leans back in her chair.

I wince in her direction. "Sorry."

"Worst dinner party ever." She tosses her napkin on the table.

"I love you," I tell him, holding his head in my hands, and kiss him again. "I love you, and it's scary, but I want everyone to know."

"I love you." He slides back. "Time to get off the table though."

I laugh and so does Warner as he helps me off and I stand in front of him. "I was so stupid to push you away."

"No, I was the stupid one. I was demanding something from you that you weren't ready to give."

"But I should've been. I should've been ready." I wrap my arms around his neck.

"Maybe if it doesn't work out between the two of you, you can get my number from Ford," Marc says. "Do you guys mind if I stick around?"

"Sure, Doc, what the hell," Aiden says from across the table.

I'm so busy kissing the love of my life, happy to have him back, that I forgot there's another thing I have to do tonight

—until Ford's chair topples over behind him when he stands.

"What the hell is going on?" Ford shouts.

"Want me to handle this?" Warner asks me.

I shake my head. "No. This was my job a long time ago." I stand in front of Warner as though I need to block him from Ford, then turn and face my big brother. "I love Warner. And you can't forbid me to date him. You can't control me like that."

"Control?" Ford's brows furrow.

"Yes. You're doing to me exactly what Dad did to you all those years, and you know how much you resented him for it. I don't want to resent you." I look at Ford with tears in my eyes because I know his protectiveness comes from a good place, but he has to let me live my life.

"No, I'm not."

Lena comes up to his side and touches his arm. When he looks at his wife, she nods. The color drains from Ford's face at my comparison of him to our father and he rubs his chest as though it aches.

"I am? But he's the bad guy. He hurt you."

"And I've forgiven him, but what you did—not allowing him to see me in the hospital—was wrong too. He had to grieve. We had to grieve together."

"But he didn't want it," Ford just about whispers.

"That's not true," Warner says. "I was taken by surprise. I was eighteen. I had nothing to my name, and I was lost when she told me she was pregnant. It was a knee-jerk reaction, but I came to my senses the next day. But by then, she'd had the miscarriage, and you blackmailed me out of her life."

The growls from the others at the table tell me that Warner has some real friends here.

"I needed you to stay away," Ford says.

"Why? It wasn't your decision." I step closer to him.

He looks around the room. "We were best friends. The day I walked in on you two, I wanted to beat the shit out of you both because I was afraid of what would happen. Look what did happen! I had to choose! Choose between the best friend I'd ever known and my sister."

"I never asked you to choose," I tell him with tears in my eyes.

"Imogen, only an asshole brother would remain friends with the guy who knocked up his sister and broke her heart by suggesting she terminate the pregnancy. If he was some other girl's boyfriend, I wouldn't have given one shit. So excuse me for not wanting you two to make up only for me to have to choose again someday."

"Ford..." Warner says from behind me.

Ford puts his hand in the air. "And now here you are on my hockey team all over again. Getting together with my friends, and now you're with my sister again. It's like fucking déjà vu."

Warner places his hand on my arm. "Let me talk to him?"

I purse my lips and nod.

"Let's go out back," he says to Ford, who surprisingly agrees.

Well, whatever happens, Warner can't say it's not all out there anymore.

CHAPTER 27

"I'm not ready to be an uncle yet!"

Warner

Ford follows me onto Drake's patio.

"What do you want?" I ask, heading directly to the bar.

"Another scotch," he says.

I pour myself a vodka tonic and him a scotch before walking over to the edge of the patio where it overlooks the beach.

"I never told you thank you," I say, passing him his drink.

Ford looks at me warily. "Thanks for what?"

"You were the first person to befriend me at Lauder, and you stayed by my side when all that shit came out about my family. I never thanked you."

He swirls the liquid in his glass. "We had a pretty great friendship. Without sounding girly or cheesy about it." He rolls his eyes.

I chuckle. "We did. And I'm sorry for letting all the stuff with Imogen get between us. I should've been a better friend. I should've told you as soon as I started having feelings for her. There's a million should haves." I look at my glass and shake my head.

"There's a million on my end too." He sips his scotch.

"But you should know... I've lived the past decade recounting all my regrets from that time in my life, and I've decided I'll never pretend to be someone I'm not. I won't be intimidated and not ask for something I want. Which means I don't give a shit if you're on board with me dating Imogen."

He laughs.

"If she's willing to forgive me and move forward, that's all I need."

He grips his glass tighter. "I didn't really think you'd stay away from her this time around. My only hope was to keep Imogen away from you." He exhales and rests his forearms on the deck, staring at the ocean. "I think I was mad back then because you were getting everything I wanted. Well, minus the girlfriend. Not only because she's my sister but because I didn't want a girlfriend." He chuckles. "I wanted the draft. I wanted to play professional hockey and not have to go to college. As fucked up as it sounds, I wanted to have a dad and mom who dreamed of having an NHL player, like you did."

"You had everything, including a billion-dollar company, ready to be handed down to you. A great family, money, most popular kid at school. How could you ever want the nothing kind of life I had?"

He sips his scotch again. "No one dictated what your future looked like. No one held their power and money over you. That was pretty damn appealing to me at eighteen years old. I was already mad that you were irresponsible enough to get my sister pregnant, and when Imogen told me what you'd said, I just saw red. I saw a guy who'd lied to me twice and was about to leave my sister after getting what he wanted from her. I convinced myself you were like every other asshole at Lauder."

I shake my head emphatically. "That wasn't it. I was scared. I felt like if Imogen had our baby, it would break us. I had a whole picture in my head of how our lives would go and it wasn't becoming parents as teenagers. She was way too young, and I didn't know how the hell I could start my hockey career off on the right foot when I had to learn how to be a parent. But before I found out she'd had a miscarriage, I was going to tell her I was all in, because a hard life with Imogen is better than any other life without her. I just needed her to be happy. I still do." I take a healthy swig of my vodka tonic, wishing we could've had this conversation ten years ago.

"We both wanted what the other had?" Ford asks.

"I think we're pretty damn lucky. To be standing here with everything we ever wanted in life." I set the glass on the ledge.

"Technically, you don't."

I look at him.

"You don't have my permission to date Imogen."

I shake my head. "You cocky motherfucker."

He turns to me and holds out his hand. "You have it. I shouldn't have kept her from you all those years ago. I was wrong. I'd like to think I've grown as a person since then, but maybe not as much as I thought, given how I've treated you since you joined the Fury. Just don't fuck this up."

I take his hand and we shake. "I'm going to marry her."

He nods with a sigh. "I know." He gestures for me to pick up my glass, then he clinks his with mine. "And I'll be your fucking best man."

"You haven't been asked."

"I know you'll ask me." He gave me his classic smirk. The one he gave me the first day I met him. The one that told me we'd be friends. "It was like an arrow to the heart when she said I was being like my dad. Fuck." He rubs his chest with his hand.

"She's right though."

"Yeah, I guess maybe I gotta talk to Paisley. I don't want Annabelle growing up like that."

"So, we're good?" I ask.

"I guess you'll find out when I pass you the puck."

"Speaking of which, how selfish can you be? We could have way more wins, but you had to be stubborn." I finish my vodka tonic and set the glass down.

"I didn't want to like you again."

"It's as simple as that?"

He laughs. "As simple as that."

I look in the house and see Imogen talking with the girls. I'm pretty sure this is the first time they heard everything that went down between us, and I'm sure they have questions. But they'll have to wait.

I clamp Ford on the shoulder. "I'm taking your sister home now."

"Fuck, can we put down some rules on PDA?"

"Sure. I'll tell you what, you don't touch Lena, and I won't touch Imogen."

"Fuck you."

I laugh and walk into the house, Ford following behind me. Imogen smiles at me, and I hold out my hand for her to join me. She accepts it freely.

"He's good?" she asks.

I look at Ford, who still looks a little pale. "He's good." Then I turn to face the group. "Sorry we're leaving the party early, but I'm taking my girlfriend home."

I kiss her cheek and everyone awws. Well, the women do.

"I'm not ready to be an uncle yet!" Ford shouts as we make our way to the front door, and everyone laughs.

I turn around, still holding Imogen's hand. "Hey, I'm an uncle now. Uncle Warner. I like the sound of that."

"No ring. No uncle." Ford points at me.

"Technicality."

He flips me off. I forgot how fun it is to rile up Ford.

Once we reach my SUV, Imogen waits a second before she climbs in. "He really is good?"

"He really is. We might even be friends again one day."

"I hope so."

I know Imogen desperately wants that, which is why I knew I had to talk to Ford. We had to reconcile if Imogen was going to have a happy life. Especially with Annabelle. But I hope to have my friend back in my life too. I'd be lying if I said I didn't.

IMOGEN'S phone rings at the crack of dawn, waking us after a night of lovemaking.

"Don't answer it," I say.

"It's Jana." She slides up to the headboard and puts it on speaker. "Good morning."

"Was this Warner's doing?"

"What?" Imogen looks at me.

I snicker, closing my eyes and feigning sleep.

"Go look at his Instagram feed," she says. "I swear, all this money being thrown at him and the minute you two become official..."

Imogen sighs and I turn my face up to her.

On my Instagram feed, I uploaded a picture I took of her when she wasn't paying attention. The caption reads, "Meet the woman behind all my smiles, all my laughs, and my entire future." Then I tagged her in the photo.

"I'm sorry, Jana, I can't even be upset." Imogen gives me a warm smile.

"You shouldn't be. And I can admit when I am wrong. People are loving it. Some say they've been calling it for weeks with the number of times they've seen you together. One mom commented ten times that she and her friends saw you at the theater." Jana huffs. "Congratulations. Tell me the whole story sometime."

"I will." She burrows under the covers with me.

"Get some sleep, Langley. Now that you've ruined your sex appeal, you better play your ass off tonight."

Jana hangs up and Imogen nuzzles into my arms.

"That was a very romantic gesture," she says.

"I told you I wanted the world to know."

"I wouldn't say you're so popular that the entire world knows."

I get on top of her, tickling her. She squirms, begging for mercy, and I kiss her. "I love you."

"Not more than I love you."

We hold each other and end up falling asleep. When I wake up a few hours later, Imogen isn't in bed. I go to look for her and find her in the spare bedroom of my house, sitting on the edge of the bed by the nightstand.

"I don't have any sex toys in that nightstand," I say, walking into the room.

She sits back on her ankles and stares at me. "I found something."

"Shit, I told her it was over, I promise." I hold up both hands and sit down beside her.

She shakes her head and pulls something from behind her back.

"What do you have there?" I ask.

But I already know. I had considered showing her myself, but I wanted her to believe in me on her own, not show her the proof that I had changed my mind all those years ago.

"The ultrasound pic of our baby." She looks at it and I hope it doesn't make her upset. "And this little Renegades onesie."

I pick up both items from her hands. "I was going to tell you."

After my interview with the Renegades, I had calmed down enough to realize that I wanted our baby. So I bought the onesie to take to her. But by the next day, Imogen was in the hospital and I didn't see her again for years. I couldn't bear to get rid of the photo and the onesie, though, so they've followed me from city to city ever since.

"I'm sure you were."

"I wanted you to believe in me on my own."

She crawls into my lap and takes the items from my hands. "Can we maybe skip some steps? I don't want to waste any more time than we already have."

"What does that mean?"

"How about I move in here, we make a baby, and then maybe get married? Pick up where we left off."

I kiss her cheek. "Did you want the baby before you found those items?"

She turns in my arms to straddle my lap, and I wrap her in my arms. "I've wanted to have your baby since way before then. And spending time with my niece hasn't hurt either."

"Okay."

"Okay?" She pulls her head back a bit to look at me.

"You sound surprised?"

"It's just a lot."

"I just want to make you half as happy as you make me." I lean in and kiss her forehead.

"Oh, I'm there. I'm so there. I can't wait for our life together." She kisses me and hugs me tightly.

"Let me guess, this room would be the nursery?"

"Is this house big enough? Because I plan on a basketball team, at least."

"Five kids?" I raise my eyebrows.

"Baseball more your style?"

"Sure, nine sounds like the magic number." I roll my eyes.

"I'll move in here. You seem kind of attached to me."

"I do? Okay. I'm not arguing with you about that."

I hold her, never wanting to know again what my arms would feel like without her. "Now you can wear my jersey to the game, right?"

Her laughter makes her chest rock against mine. "You bet. I've already got my outfit planned out."

"Good. We have an appointment at the tattoo parlor in twenty."

She pulls back and looks at me with wide eyes. "Tattoo parlor?"

"Yeah, to have my number tattooed on both cheeks."

"Stop it." She playfully smacks my chest.

We get up off the bed and I carry her back to our bedroom. We leave the ultrasound and outfit from our first baby in the spare room, where we're sure to bring another baby home soon.

"We're going to fill our house with laughter, aren't we?" she asks.

"Love and laughter and you." I kiss her, dropping her on the mattress.

Her laugh rings out through the house, and I can't wait to hear many little voices of laughter mixed in one day soon.

EPILOGUE

"I thought we agreed."
_{—Imogen}

Imogen

Four Months Later...

"Finally, you passed the puck. Way to play well with others." I pat my brother's head as he leaves the locker room after practice, but he dodges out of my way.

"I've been passing it to your boyfriend for a while now."

"And now we're finally winning," Aiden says.

The rest of the boys come out of the locker room. We're getting together at our place for a huge cookout today, and everyone is responsible for one dish.

"Hey, you here by yourself?" a deep voice asks from behind me. He wraps his arms around my stomach. A silent sign no one else will notice.

I'm only six weeks pregnant and we want to wait until we're sure everything is okay before we tell anyone, although the doctor says everything looks good right now. I still can't believe Warner was okay with us planning a pregnancy before marriage. He's usually so traditional.

Last week, we flew up to visit his mom, Trinity, and Julien, who are now thinking maybe they want to relocate to Florida. It might've been a push from me. I'm big on family, and the way the boys are playing together now, I don't see anyone being traded somewhere else. At least, I hope so.

"My boyfriend is really big and protective. We better get out of here before he catches us." I take Warner's hand and pull him along, but he drops his bag and picks me up, kissing me so thoroughly my cheeks are red when he sets me down.

"Your niece wants you to stop kissing in public." Ford holds Annabelle up toward us.

I take Annabelle from his arms. "I doubt that. Always pick a boy who wears his heart on his sleeve. Who wants to show the world you're his." I poke her tummy and she giggles.

"Believe me, people in Tibet know you're his girlfriend." Ford rolls his eyes.

I wave him off. "Whatever."

"Who needs to go to the store? Let's meet over at our house in, like, two hours?" Warner says to the group.

"A few of us are going to the store now if anyone wants to join us," I say.

"I'm gonna go home and make sure everything is good to go. I think I have to get some propane and stuff. I'll meet you there." Warner places a chaste kiss on my lips.

"I say the guys go home and the girls go to the store," Ford suggests.

"Except for Cory. He can come with us." I smile at the rookie.

Everyone has been on a mission to fix Cory up. He's taken ladies man to a new level lately and earned himself a little reputation with the ladies. But he's so cute and we all want him to find happiness. We tried to fix up Kane too, but he's not having it.

"I don't want to practice meeting women at the grocery store," Cory whines.

"Let's just see what it has to offer. Saige was reading an article the other day about how many people meet their future spouses there." Paisley smiles at him.

Cory groans, but he's so nice. Of course he allows us to have our fun with him.

"I have to get Annabelle ready. So I'll just meet you at your place." Lena waves goodbye.

Ten minutes later, the girls and Cory and I are at the grocery store with lists of what we need.

"I'm going to the premade items," Cory says and leaves us behind.

"All the more reason you need to find someone," Saige calls after him.

I'm in the produce section grabbing the limes for the beer when I do a double take. Hurriedly, I grab my phone from my purse and scroll through my pictures from Ford and Lena's wedding in the tropics. Sure enough, I'm right.

I hammer out a group text to the girls.

Me: *The girl from the wedding is here! Cory's girl! Produce section ASAP*

No one responds, which doesn't surprise me. They aren't going to waste time. And just like that, Saige comes from one direction, Tedi and Paisley from another.

The woman places a bag of salad mix in her almost empty cart.

"That's her." I show them my phone.

Cory puts a rotisserie chicken in his basket—for what, I have no idea. He really needs a woman. But at the exact same moment, they look up and see one another.

"OMG." Tedi claps. "I thought she lived somewhere else?"

"Salt Lake City." Saige acts as if she's hiding behind me.

The woman giggles.

"That's a good sign. She laughed at something he said," I say to the girls.

We inch closer to hear better, tiptoeing like the most unprofessional spies you've ever seen.

"What did she say?" Paisley asks, squatting behind the banana display.

"That she moved, I think." I'm squinting as though that'll help me hear better.

"Ande, that's her name. I just heard him say it," Saige says.

"Oh, he just asked her to the cookout." Tedi leans in closer but loses her footing and grabs for the orange stand to stop herself from falling. But it doesn't hold her weight and the entire display topples, oranges rolling everywhere.

Cory and Ande look at us.

I offer a small wave. "We thought that was you."

"Help, I can't get up," Paisley says. "Doctor Marc was right about heels. My arches are really letting me down these days."

Saige helps Paisley up and we go over to say hello. Cory looks completely annoyed.

"You should come to Imogen's. She dates Warner Langley now," Tedi says.

Ande laughs. "I saw."

"Their billboard, you mean. Yeah, he can just stop now." Tedi puts her finger in her mouth.

I blush because I love that Warner likes to show me off. No, he didn't put up a billboard, but I'm plastered all over his social media almost more than he is.

"Well, I'd love to, but..." Ande stops, and we all wait for her to continue.

Cory groans.

"You know what? We have to go. I forgot Warner wants sausage. Big, thick sausage," I say.

"Nice." Ande smiles.

"Did you hear yourself?" Tedi pushes me forward while saying to Cory and Ande, "We'll meet you at the cashier. Hope to see you there."

We all walk away, trying not to be any weirder than we already were.

"I'm sorry. I think of my boyfriend and the first thing on my mind is big, thick sausages," I say.

Fifteen minutes later, we're at the cashier and Cory meets us there with Ande and some other guy.

Tedi leans in close to Cory. "What's up with the tagalong with a dick?"

"It's her boyfriend," Cory grinds out.

"I can't believe you know someone who plays for the Fury, Ande. Why didn't you ever tell me?" the guy says to her.

Tedi's eyebrows crinkle in confusion at Cory.

"Girls, this is my boyfriend, Trevor. Trevor, these are all the girlfriends of..."

"Imogen Jacobs, you date Warner Langley," Trevor says, pointing at me with a big smile.

"That's like the free bingo marker. Try another one of us," Tedi says.

He shrugs. "I just saw the Instagram post."

"You and everyone else." Tedi rolls her eyes.

"Hey now, there's no reason to be so snippy about him loving me. Don't we want the best for one another?"

Paisley puts her hand on my shoulder. "Of course, sweetie."

We introduce ourselves and Trevor seems over the moon

about getting to meet all the hockey players this afternoon. And he clearly has no idea he's standing next to the one member of the Florida Fury who fucked Ande's brains out last summer.

I give Ande our address and tell them they can follow us to the house while the rest of us drive over in the one car. Tedi badgers Cory with question after question. He doesn't seem too inclined to answer them though. Probably because he appears really pissed off.

I'm thankful when we reach the house, but there are a lot of cars in the driveway and on the street. I swear we only invited a select few players. Then again, Warner can get carried away sometimes.

"We got this. Imogen, you head in and play hostess to your guests," Saige says.

"That's silly. Give me a bag or the watermelon."

"You're not carrying a watermelon. Go on and we'll be right behind you." Paisley pushes me forward.

I walk into the house and hear "Dance with Me" by Morgan Evans playing.

"Warner?" I call, but no one answers.

There's a note on the counter, folded in half with my name in his handwriting. I lift it and read it.

Come meet me outside, please.

I hold the card as I walk outside to our porch and pool that overlooks the beach. I shake my head, seeing Warner at the end of a long line of our friends and family. Even the girls and Cory must've run from the other side of the house. There are candlelit lanterns along the sand even though it's only dusk, and flowers run the length of the path. Warner's barefoot but dressed in slacks and an untucked button-down shirt.

Slowly, I walk to him, looking at everyone we love, from

my parents to his mom and our siblings and the family of teammates we've made here. Even Cici is here.

"You owe me big. I told you this day was coming," she whispers when I pass her.

I reach Warner, tears in my eyes. "I thought we agreed." My voice is soft.

He leans forward and whispers in my ear, "I just don't want any mix-ups at the hospital. Better if we all have the same name."

I shake my head and he chuckles, taking my hands.

"I wanted to write 'hurry' on that card, but I thought it would be perceived wrong. It's just we lost so much time together and sometimes I feel like we're running to catch up. That's why you're the perfect partner for me. I can stand here and promise you the world if you agree to marry me, but the truth is we both know it doesn't matter if you marry me or not, I'll give you the world anyway. This is just a formality, so we can put up one of those cute signs outside our house that says The Langleys."

Everyone laughs, and I do too.

"Actually, I just want to make sure if you ever want to leave me, you'll think about all the paperwork involved and wonder if it's worth it."

Everyone laughs again.

Warner squeezes my hands. "In all seriousness, my life is nothing without you. All of my happiness is wrapped up in you, and I think we can have one helluva life together. What do you say? Go on a journey with me, and if we're lucky, at the end we'll be more in love than we are right now." He drops to his knee and pulls out a box with a sizable round diamond nestled in platinum. "You're already my every-thing, but will you be my wife, Gen?"

"Yes." My tears spill over, and I drop to my knees too. He

slides the ring on my left ring finger. "I love it." I lean forward and kiss him. "You surprised me."

We both stand as he says, "You know how hard that is to accomplish?"

I hug him and kiss him once more before our family and friends surround us to offer their congratulations.

It means the most when Ford takes each of us into an embrace. "Congratulations, you two. I'm glad you found each other again."

"Thanks, big brother."

He gives me another hug, then goes in search of Annabelle when he hears her cry.

We go down the row and it's like a wedding receiving line. But when we get to the end where Ande and Trevor are, Warner leans in.

"I didn't invite these two," he murmurs.

"Honey, you remember Ande from that tropical island we were on for Ford's wedding?"

Although it wasn't that long ago, Warner wasn't invited, and it was a whole complicated mess that put us at the same resort as one another, but I can't very well call her Cory's Ande in front of her boyfriend.

"Sure." Warner goes along with it.

"This is Ande and her boyfriend, Trevor."

"Nice to see you again," Ande says.

We shake hands and walk away.

Warner turns to me. "I'm so confused."

"That was Cory's Ande, and that was Ande's boyfriend. So what happened in between, you figure out." I shrug.

"Fuck, poor Cory," he says.

"Yep. Now let's go upstairs for a quickie before the party gets rolling."

He picks me up bride style and runs up the beach as I laugh and yelp.

We might have veered off course for a while, but we found our way back to each other. In the end, that's all that matters.

The End

Cockamamie Unicorn Ramblings

There was lot more to Warner than we'd originally planned. We knew he'd be Ford's best friend in high school, and obviously would've been a love interest for Imogen. But throughout books #1 and #2 in the Hockey Hotties, that's all we knew. Then when we got to Ford's book and Imogen came on page more, we knew we had to set something up, so we dug deeper.

Making Warner not come from money seemed like the sensible way to go. He wasn't like his classmates in that he had a rougher childhood and fought for everything he got. It was the perfect primer for him having to fight to win Imogen back, right?

Other than not making Warner another trust fund baby like Ford, there were small things we changed along the way... like Ford not caring so much that Warner and Imogen got together when they were younger and the kids at school assuming he came from a wealthy family and Warner deciding to go along with that.

Oh! And we played with the idea of making Imogen think she might be pregnant again at the end but we scraped it because by then Warner and Imogen believed in one another's love again. And we really wanted to write the dinner scene because what's better than watching Warner squirm because he's jealous!?

A surprise while writing would have to be how devastated Ford was by what went down in the past. Although what happened all those years ago hurt Imogen and Warner, it hurt Ford, too.

Without our team you wouldn't have any of our books! Seriously, they take on a lot of the work off our hands so that we can write! Or procrastinate. Whatever. ;)

Danielle Sanchez and the entire Wildfire Marketing Solutions team.

Cassie from Joy Editing for line edits.

Ellie from My Brother's Editor for line edits.

Rosa from My Brother's Editor for proofreading.

Hang Le for the cover and branding for the entire series. Those colors!

Wander Aguiar for our muse.

Bloggers who consistently carve out time to read, review and/or promote our work.

Piper Rayne Unicorns who love our characters like as much as we do! Thank you!

Readers who took the time to read our story when there's so many choices out there.

Now you got Cory and Ande's story, Second Shot with #76, coming next. You haven't seen them a ton, but this rookie might get the break of a lifetime. We hope so because he's got something to prove if he intends to win Ande's heart.

xo,

Piper & Rayne

ABOUT PIPER & RAYNE

Piper Rayne is a USA Today Bestselling Author duo who write "heartwarming humor with a side of sizzle" about families, whether that be blood or found. They both have e-readers full of one-clickable books, they're married to husbands who drive them to drink, and they're both chauffeurs to their kids. Most of all, they love hot heroes and quirky heroines who make them laugh, and they hope you do, too!

ALSO BY PIPER RAYNE

Hockey Hotties

My Lucky #13

The Trouble with #9

Faking it with #41

Sneaking around with #34

Second Shot with #76

Offside with #55

Kingsmen Football Stars

You had your chance, Lee Burrows

You can't kiss the Nanny, Brady Banks

Over my Brother's Dead Body, Chase Andrews

The Baileys

Lessons from a One-Night Stand

Advice from a Jilted Bride

Birth of a Baby Daddy

Operation Bailey Wedding (Novella)

Falling for My Brother's Best Friend

Demise of a Self-Centered Playboy

Confessions of a Naughty Nanny

Operation Bailey Babies (Novella)

Secrets of the World's Worst Matchmaker

Winning My Best Friend's Girl

Rules for Dating your Ex

Operation Bailey Birthday (Novella)

The Greenes

My Beautiful Neighbor

My Almost Ex

My Vegas Groom

The Greene Family Summer Bash

My Sister's Flirty Friend

My Unexpected Surprise

My Famous Frenemy

The Greene Family Vacation

My Scorned Best Friend

My Fake Fiancé

My Brother's Forbidden Friend

The Modern Love World

Charmed by the Bartender

Hooked by the Boxer

Mad about the Banker

The Single Dad's Club

Real Deal

Dirty Talker

Sexy Beast

Hollywood Hearts

Mister Mom

Animal Attraction

Domestic Bliss

Bedroom Games

Cold as Ice

On Thin Ice

Break the Ice

Box Set

Charity Case

Manic Monday

Afternoon Delight

Happy Hour

Blue Collar Brothers

Flirting with Fire

Crushing on the Cop

Engaged to the EMT

White Collar Brothers

Sexy Filthy Boss

Dirty Flirty Enemy

Wild Steamy Hook-up

The Rooftop Crew

My Bestie's Ex

A Royal Mistake

The Rival Roomies

Our Star-Crossed Kiss

The Do-Over

A Co-Workers Crush

www.ingramcontent.com/pod-product-compliance
Lightning Source LLC
Chambersburg PA
CBHW020149310726
48970CB00006B/2072